LUNA CONFLICTED

BOOK 3 OF THE LUNA RISING SERIES (A PARANORMAL SHIFTER ROMANCE SERIES)

SARA SNOW

RUBY

*H*ave you ever been stabbed? Have you ever felt anything razor-sharp piercing into your body, tearing through skin and flesh? Do you have any idea how excruciating that is?

I could feel the man's pointed fangs slicing through my skin as if I was made of butter. I could feel his curved claws digging into my shoulders as he held me down to feed on me. I listened in abject horror as he slurped noisily on my blood.

So, this is how I die—being slurped on like a milkshake?

I screamed. My wide eyes that had been glued to the dark sky above in fright screwed tightly shut as I screamed for my life. I could feel my body growing weaker and weaker, the more he fed on me. My screams were muffled as he covered my mouth and forced my head to the side.

Xavier, Axel...are they dead?

Are they being fed on the way I am?

I could feel my tears sliding from my eyes. When I opened them, I could barely see the world around me now as blurry as an impressionist painting. I could still feel the pain in my neck, but it felt almost distant. I was dying.

That was when it appeared–a shadow above the vampire. He was too busy feeding on me to notice it.

My eyelids felt like they were being weighed down by an anchor and though I tried, I couldn't call out to the shadow for help. I couldn't even move.

The vampire pressed down on my face and the world around me finally faded away.

I bolted upright, my hand gripping my chest as I gasped for breath. I started looking around me frantically, my eyes wide and my body shivering.

I was in a room, a dark room. For a second, I thought maybe it had all been a dream until my hand flew to my neck. My shoulders slumped as I felt the bandage there. Unfortunately, it had not been a dream, but instead a real-life nightmare.

Xavier. Axel.

The names echoed in my mind and I looked around the semi-dark room once more as I got out of the bed.

Where am I?

My only hope was that whoever saved me also saved Xavier and Axel as well. I had too many questions and no one to answer them. I decided to look for someone.

The hallway was dark, but I could see light down the hall coming from a room. The tiles were cold under my feet, my steps slow as I walked on my toes to prevent any sound of my approach. Whoever it was in that room might not be friendly. I still didn't know why that person saved me, or what their intentions were.

I stopped walking as I held onto the oversized shirt I was

wearing. *Maybe it's the Council. Maybe they caught up with us just in time to save my life.* But if it was the Council that saved me, then my survival was merely temporary. After they got what they wanted from me, my life would still come to an end, just at their hands instead. *I need to find the guys. I hope they are alive to be found.* My chest tightened at the thought and I clenched my fists.

What was that man that bit me? I thought to myself as I continued walking. There had been just enough light for me to see his pale skin and crimson eyes. I still knew so little about the supernatural community, I could only guess that maybe he was a demon or a vampire. No, he couldn't have been. If Axel and Xavier couldn't tell what was hunting us by its scent, no way could he be a vampire. They would know what a demon or vampire smelled like, right?

From what I understood, werewolves used to act as protectors, assuming the role of watchdogs - no pun intended - for both the humans and the supernatural world alike. Now only some packs chose to function as guardians. Like Xavier's pack–they hunted down supernaturals who sought to create havoc or do harm. So wouldn't Xavier know any supernatural creature well enough by its scent?

Whispering voices met my ears as I drew closer to the door.

"We don't have a choice. We have to tell the others because they will be back. This will buy us time with the Council."

I felt a pang of relief as I made out Axel's voice, and then I frowned. Why was I so concerned for him? I rolled my eyes. I certainly was unhappy with his behavior towards me, but I didn't want anything serious to happen to him. Deep down, some part of me felt relieved he'd survived the attack.

"Once Ruby wakes up, we'll leave. Not before."

I closed my eyes and sighed as I heard Xavier speak. I walked into the room. Their gazes turned to me, but my eyes fell on a man standing to the left of the room.

His grey eyes found mine and he gave me a warm smile.

I returned it and looked away. "What's going on? What happened?"

Xavier walked over to me, his eyes glistening as he guided me to a chair. "Sit." He nodded almost imperceptibly at the grey-eyed man and then he backed away.

The stranger then moved to approach me, a strand of yellow blonde hair falling onto his forehead as he bent down.

I pulled away somewhat as the unknown man reached out to me.

He paused. "I'm only going to check your wound."

I looked at Xavier and then Axel, who had his arms crossed over his chest. I frowned because there was a thin pink line running from his left cheek down to his neck. No doubt, a wound he had suffered at the hands of the unknown supernatural that had already healed.

I exhaled and allowed the man to remove the bandage from my neck, wincing somewhat as the tape pulled at my skin.

He nodded as he stepped back. "All healed."

"Already?" Xavier asked, and Axel moved forward to see my neck. A look passed between them.

I reached up and touched the area. True enough, I was healed. The area felt completely smooth as if nothing had happened. I couldn't feel any evidence of the horrible trauma

I endured, not even the raised skin of a telltale scar left behind. "Is there a mark?" I asked.

The man shook his head. "There is none," he replied as he glanced at Axel and then Xavier. He crossed the room to throw my bandage in a bin.

I watched him with narrowed eyes. *Who is he? Where the hell were we, anyway? How long had I been asleep in order for my wound to have healed completely? And how could I have healed without so much as a mark?* That man—creature had ripped into my throat.

I hadn't realized I had been slowly massaging the area until Xavier held my hand. It was as if I could still feel something there, despite being healed.

"How are you feeling?" he asked me, as he looked me up and down.

Suddenly aware that I was wearing nothing except a large T-shirt barely reaching my knees, my cheeks began to heat. "I feel fine." I pulled my hand away and interlocked my fingers on my lap. "I feel fine, just kind of in shock, I guess. What attacked us? How long have I been sleeping?"

Xavier sat down across from me while Axel remained standing, his hazel eyes piercing into me.

I still couldn't understand why I was so panicked when he'd been yanked out of the car. I'd felt a stab of fear so strong, I could barely think. I don't want to care about him, but apparently, that isn't completely under my conscious control. Some part of me did care about Axel, whether I wanted to or not. When had this happened? Would I have ever known how much I cared about Axel if we hadn't been placed in a life or death situation? How could I have feelings for a man who once almost yanked my hair out from the root as he dragged me out of his dungeon?

Maybe because he showed you he wasn't a complete asshole by leaving with you and Xavier, thereby putting himself and his pack at risk.

"You've been asleep for a good while," Axel replied, his gravelly voice carried through the room. He then pinched the bridge of his nose and turned away. "We were attacked by vampires."

So, I was right after all.

I studied Xavier thoughtfully, taking in his beautiful face. As his eyes hadn't left me since I walked into this room. I thought I had lost him when I heard him screaming as he'd faced the vampire while the pain in my heart had damn near killed me. I sighed. "Why did neither of you know that it was vampires outside the car when you first smelled them?" My eyes drifted to Axel when he turned around to stare at me. "You two panicked."

"I didn't panic," Axel retorted.

I made a face. *Who is he kidding?* "Yes, you did. I was there...remember? Why don't you guys know what vampires smell like?" I stared at Xavier, whose lips formed a thin line, and I frowned. The room was filled with silence and my eyes found the blonde man who'd been listening to our conversation quietly.

He was holding his chin, a finger gliding back and forth over his lips.

No one seemed interested in answering me.

Axel dug his hands into his pockets.

Xavier's soothing voice licked at my ears, "This is the first time either of us has met a vampire."

Axel cleared his throat. "Vampires have been extinct for hundreds of years."

I frowned as I tilted my head to the side. "What?" The blonde man briefly drew my attention as he left the room, then I glanced back over at Axel. He'd certainly piqued my interest with that unexpected statement. *So, if vampires had been extinct for hundreds of years, how exactly had one just ripped into my throat?*

Axel sat down and crossed his legs.

I noticed for the first time just how exhausted both Xavier and he looked.

"What we know about vamps now comes from stories told to us over the years," Xavier said. "They were said to be bloodthirsty and animalistic, with no shred of thought other than the drive to quench their ravenous thirst."

Axel sat forward, his elbows on his knees. The strands of his hair loose from his bun slid forward to cover his cheeks. "Vampires were the parasites of the earth. Their only purpose was to exist, feed, and populate."

An image of the vampire that attacked me appeared in my mind as Axel spoke and a chill passed through my body.

"Their thirst for blood, any and every creature's blood, is insatiable," Axel went on. "As a result, they lived as outcasts. They belonged to no community, supernatural or otherwise, because they contaminated and killed everything they came into contact with. Years ago, werewolves, humans, and several other supernaturals banded together and waged war on them, wiping them out for good."

"Umm, I think they survived," I replied under my breath.

"Clearly." Axel nodded. "They were said to be pale, hideous creatures capable of turning any living being–

7

human, werewolf, witch, anyone–into bloodsuckers like themselves. Their venom is so strong, it is capable of completely changing one's anatomy–completely erasing who and what you are. They were among the most dangerous supernatural beings in existence." He shook his head. "Still are, apparently."

I nodded.

Xavier ran his hand down his face, pulling his cheeks down. "I can't figure out how they've survived without anyone knowing. In all the stories I've heard, no one ever mentioned that their scent is so strong. How have they masked it for so many years?"

That vampire that attacked me had indeed been pale, but he hadn't been hideous. Maybe he hadn't shown his true self? He also hadn't seemed like a bloodthirsty, thoughtless creature. Well, bloodthirsty, maybe. But thoughtless? No, I'd gotten the feeling he'd been a lot closer to a human or werewolf in thoughts and motivations than Axel and Xavier's stories were depicting. "So, what are we going to do?" I asked as I looked at them both.

"We have no choice but to go back home," Xavier replied as he tapped a finger on the arm of the chair.

"No," I said as I shook my head. "I can't go back. The two of you know I can't. Vampires or not, the Council wants me dead. Have you both forgotten that?"

Axel huffed. "Forgotten it? It's the reason we left. It's the reason we were attacked by vampires. How can we forget, Ruby? You need to remember that they want Xavier and me dead as well now. This isn't only about you."

"Axel," Xavier said in a warning tone.

I bit my lip and looked away. Axel was right. My life

wasn't the only one on the line here, but I was scared. Not only was I running from the all-powerful werewolf Council, but now there were vampires on the loose out there, ones that even intimidated two full-grown male werewolves.

These two men were alphas-to-be. In fact, Axel was an alpha in all but name. Yet, they had their asses handed to them when they'd faced off against that vamp. Sure, it had been a full moon, and they had been caught off guard. But still, I did feel terrified of anything that could strike fear into these two men. I didn't know about the guys, but I wasn't interested in becoming some vampire's lunch, or worse, getting turned into a vamp myself.

"Ruby?"

I looked Xavier's way as my name glided off his lips like honey.

"This new threat, it's very serious," he said. "If vampires are back and we know they are, this means trouble. We have to warn my dad and the Council. Other packs need to know this. I don't know much about vampires, but if the stories are true, then the entire world is in danger."

"The stories are true," Axel added. "Even if they have been altered over time, the danger vampires pose is real. They are savages, and because of their infectious bite, they multiply quickly. We don't know how many people were turned before we were attacked."

I wanted to ask him why we couldn't simply call Mathieu and warn him, but I knew that would be selfish. I'd been lucky to survive being bitten...I knew this. If vampires decided to attack now, how many more would die if they maintained their element of surprise? "Okay," I replied as I scratched at my brow and closed my eyes. I quickly reopened them when I started to get a flashback of the vampire as he attacked me, his glistening white fangs aimed directly at my throat. "Okay," I repeated, as I rolled my shoulders and sat up straight. "We do need to warn everyone."

Axel sat back and reclined in his seat, his eyes lowering into slits. "There's a book that has been in my family for generations. Supposedly, it holds the history of werewolves and other supernatural beings. I was never allowed to look inside it as a child. In fact, it's been so long since I've even seen it that I'd almost forgotten about it." He looked back and forth between the two of us, a contemplative look on his face. "It contains information on vampires, their weaknesses, and how to fight them. Any knowledge we can gain from it about vampires will be helpful since we know so little right now."

At this point, I was barely listening to him. My mind had taken me back to that highway, to the moment when I felt my blood gushing from my neck as that vampire consumed it. My shoulder twitched, something like a phantom feeling still present there.

"Ruby?" Xavier called to me.

My head snapped towards him.

He stared at me with concern.

I looked away, my eyes downcast to the floor. "I thought I was going to die," I said under my breath. "I thought you were both dead."

"We almost were," Axel replied.

I watched him from under my lashes.

He looked angry, and I could understand why. He wasn't someone that liked feeling out of control—this much I knew. He got his ass kicked and I could only imagine the level of his rage right now. The severity of the cut on his face under-scored just how close of a call it had been.

"Who was he?" I asked. "The shadow. You know the person that saved us? Did either of you see him?" I lowered my voice. "Was it blondie?"

Axel frowned as he rose to stretch.

The action struck me as odd. It seemed too mundane coming from Axel. I supposed he must be tired. He certainly looked tired, anyways. Why did it seem as if neither Xavier nor he had rested the way I had? I glanced over at Xavier.

He'd been propping his head up with his hand, his eyes staring ahead. He appeared lost in thought.

I realized he'd barely spoken. "How long have we been here?"

His eyes shifted to me. "We've been here for two days."

"Blondie, as you called him," Axel interjected. "Wasn't the one that saved us. We're at my safe house right now, and he's the warlock I hired to watch the place. He keeps the place protected with warding. Whoever saved us and killed those vamps, got us here in a matter of hours."

I frowned as my eyes widened.

"He said there was a knock at the door and when he opened it, we were lying on the ground outside." Axel pointed at my neck. "Your wound was already almost healed and only bleeding a little. The same goes for us and our wounds. I, for one, feel drained. That fucker almost drained me."

I understood now, that's why they looked so beaten.

"On the other hand, you seem to have recovered rather quickly, especially for a human," Axel continued as he studied me suspiciously. "A little warlock magic was needed, but I would have expected your wounds to have healed slower. Your blood count would certainly take some additional time to replenish."

My eyes narrowed at his tone and the way he was staring at me. I shrugged, not sure what to say to him. How was I to answer that? "Considering this was my first time having my neck ripped open by a vampire, I don't know what to tell you. We can compare how fast I heal if it ever happens again."

And just like that, my anger at Axel returned.

"Whoever saved us must have done something to save Ruby first," Xavier said. "We were almost beyond the point of no return. It would have taken less effort to drain Ruby, I would assume, given her smaller size in comparison to us. Either way, I think it's clear that at least someone out there knows about these vamps and how to kill them. Were they just in the right place at the right time, or did they already know what was going to happen? And how did they know where to take us if this safe house is unknown to others, even Axel's pack?" He questioned, looking at Axel as he said it. Then Xavier stood and ran his hand down his shirt. "There are a lot of questions about how we survived. All we really know is that we did. But right now, getting back to the pack has to be our priority." He turned to leave the room and paused. "Come on," he said to me. "You need to eat."

My stomach chose that moment to growl.

2

RUBY

*S*ince we've been here for two days, that meant I'd been asleep for two days.

Xavier made me a sandwich. I immediately wolfed it down and asked for another. He finished his and vanished while I continued to munch on mine, eating much slower this time around.

He'd been quiet the whole time, and I could understand why. So much was happening. Too much was happening. At every turn so far, we collided with a wall. Every time a new solution presented itself, the walls started closing in. Before we knew it, we ended up trapped once more.

I looked down at the piece of sandwich left and pushed the plate away. I didn't see an end to this, especially now with this new vampire threat. I could feel it in my bones that things were about to get so much worse.

"Finally full, huh?"

I glanced over my shoulder at Axel, who stood leaning against the door.

His face lacked any expression as he stared at me.

I said nothing as I looked away. I closed my eyes and listened as he pulled the stool out beside me and sat down at the island with me.

When I opened my eyes, in my peripheral vision I could see him just staring at me. "What?" I asked as I tilted my head to look his way.

He didn't say anything and continued staring at me.

I held his stare with narrowed eyes. I didn't have time for this. Whatever game he was looking to play, I wasn't interested. I felt too tired and too worried to deal with his bullshit. "Seriously, Axel, what do you want? Am I sitting on your favorite stool or something?"

"How are you feeling?" he asked softly.

I stared at him. This wasn't what I was expecting, especially not from him. Was he being serious? Am I supposed to believe he actually cared? Less than an hour ago, he'd been looking at me suspiciously because I wasn't still in bed or battling for my life like he assumed a weak human should be. "I feel fine, Axel."

He tilted his head to the side. "The night we were attacked, I heard you. You didn't want to leave me behind. Why?"

Oh, for god's sake. I looked away and sighed. I picked up and ate the final piece of the sandwich, chewing slowly.

Axel rested his hand on the counter as his eyes continued to bore into me. "You were worried about me," he added.

I shook my head. "I wasn't."

"I know you're lying, Ruby." He leaned forward somewhat, his finger tapping against the counter. "I can tell because the octave in your voice changed, so you might as well tell me the truth. Why were you worried about me?"

He wasn't going to let this go…I could see that. I had no idea why he cared about this, but I didn't have an answer for him. I was too busy trying to figure it out myself. Why had I cared? He was the only reason we were running from the Council to begin with. So what if he finally realized he'd fucked up and now wanted to be on Xavier's and my side? He could switch back on us at any time. He'd made it clear multiple times that his only priorities were his position as alpha and protecting his pack.

What if he was ever given an ultimatum: protect me or to remain an alpha? I wonder how that would turn out.

I smoothed my brows down as I turned to look at him. Thinking about all of that now would neither solve nor help our current situation in any way. If it ever came to that, we'd handle it then. I'd handle it then. "I don't know," I answered truthfully. "Just let it go, okay?"

"Okay," he replied easily as he leaned away from me.

I felt like I could finally breathe again. Actually, there had been something I wanted to ask him. "How are humans turned exactly? Do you know how long it takes before they start to change?"

He turned to face the island and replied, "You don't need to worry about that. I think you would have turned by now. That vampire was only feeding." He looked suddenly lost in thought.

"Are you scared?" I asked.

He looked over at me as if I'd spoken a language he didn't understand.

I could see it in his eyes the same way I could with Xavier. This was new territory for them both.

"No," he replied.

I rolled my eyes. "Yeah, I can tell when you're lying too."

His lips curved with a small smile. "So you think you know me now?"

I peered down at his arm, noticing yet another fading red line. Another wound he must have suffered while fighting the vampires. It started from just above his elbow and went all the way down to the middle of his forearm. I couldn't imagine how painful that must have been. "You know a lot about vampires,"

He turned his body to face me once more.

I scowled a bit because I hated it when he did this. The closer he got, the harder my heart pounded. It confused me even more and knowing he could hear it didn't help matters.

His brow rose. "I said I was *told* to never look inside the book. I never said I *listened*."

I couldn't help it…I laughed. It slipped out before I could stop it. "Of course you did. You listen to nothing and no one," I chided with a smirk as I shook my head. I should have expected something like that from him.

"That's right," he replied quickly and proudly.

I rolled my eyes yet again.

"My pack is one of few that still hold wolf history close," he explained. "As the years pass, things change and things are forgotten. That can't be helped, but we must have a place where history is kept and honored. No doubt, the Council has information on vampires stored away as well, but I won't be relying on them. Olcan showed me exactly how naive I have been when it comes to the Council and how they operate. My father might know more, so I'll consult him and the book. I had my beta move him to somewhere safe after we left. Olcan can't be trusted." His jaw clenched. "I know that now."

If only he had figured that out earlier, but it was in the past. When I eavesdropped on his conversation with Olcan, he'd revealed his father was ill. "What's wrong with your dad?"

He looked angry at this question.

I raised my hands. "You don't have to tell me if you don't want to. I was just curious."

"My mother died a few years ago during childbirth," he replied. "My baby sister died with her."

My eyes widened and I bit my lip, mentally slapping myself for being nosy.

"My dad hasn't been the same since. As an alpha, he carried on for a while as best he could. But unlike Xavier's father, he wasn't able to hold his broken pieces together." His eyes began to dance over my face.

Heat began to crawl up my skin. "Do you have any other siblings?"

He shook his head. "No. It's always been just me."

I could've been wrong, but I sensed so much loneliness in that response.

Axel must have realized it as well because his eyes darkened before he looked away. He got up and walked to the fridge to grab a bottle of water.

"I, um, I wonder what happened after we left, after Olcan realized we'd left." I wasn't very subtle about trying to change the subject. "Do you think he's still there?"

He finished half of the bottle in one swig. "I guess we'll find out soon enough."

"When are we leaving?"

17

He shrugged. "In a day or so maybe," he answered before finishing the rest of the water. "It's best if Xavier and I are back to full strength before we leave."

"I saw him, you know," I offered spontaneously.

Crossing his arms over his wide chest, he leaned on the sink.

"The man that saved us, I saw him just before I fell unconscious," I went on. "I wasn't able to see his face, but I want to know who it was. Why did they save us?"

Axel didn't meet my eyes as he uncrossed his arms to hold the edge of the sink. "I want the answers to those questions as well. I hadn't smelled anyone else, which is surprising since he must have been fairly close in order to have made it in time to save us. It wasn't another wolf."

Instinctively, my hand moved to my neck again.

Turning his head towards me, his eyes were glued to my hand as it covered the spot where my wound should have been. His grip on the counter grew tighter. "Vampires have become myths. In fact, some don't even believe they ever really existed. If they attack now, so many will die. How have they survived for so long without being found?"

I truly wished I knew the answer to that. "I didn't smell what you guys did, so maybe they've been hiding around humans. Maybe in places where there are no werewolf packs that could sniff them out?"

"Perhaps," he said thoughtfully. "They would have an endless supply of food and humans to turn. I wonder just how many of them there are now if they've been in hiding for all these years."

This was a troubling thought. There could be an army of them now, scattered all over the world. I would think a full-scale attack was only a matter of time at this point. But why would they show their faces now, and to us? A thought occurred to me and I sat up straight. "They attacked us on a full moon, but the potions we had drunk were still masking our scents. Maybe they thought they were attacking humans and not werewolves."

Nodding his head at this, he stepped forward. "You're right. That must—"

"You guys need to see this," Xavier suddenly announced from the doorway then turned and walked away.

Axel and I shared a look before following him.

What now?

We followed him into the living room.

I immediately took a seat, my attention drawn to the female reporter on the television.

She stood at the scene of a gruesome crime-an entire family killed. Every single victim had been drained of their blood.

My eyes widened as I realized what she was saying. I gazed over at Axel and Xavier in shock.

Xavier changed the channel.

This time a male reporter told of a similar killing in another city – a jogger murdered in a park. This victim, too, had been drained of his blood.

Maybe they hadn't only attacked us because they hadn't been able to tell that Axel and Xavier were werewolves. They attacked us because they were making their kills more public.

"They're slowly coming out of hiding," I said as I hugged myself.

"I'd say they are coming out of hiding rather quickly,"

Axel objected. "If they continue this, the humans will become aware of them. And guess who they'll be finding next?"

"Werewolves," I said under my breath.

Axel nodded. "Not just werewolves...the entire fucking supernatural community will be discovered," he growled through clenched teeth. "No offense to you, Ruby, but humans won't be able to handle this discovery. Vampires are starting a war and they don't even know it."

"Maybe they do," Xavier stated.

Axel and I looked his way.

His eyes were glued to the television as the reporter continued to speak. "It's like you said, Axel, they're making their kills known. For years, they've remained hidden. Now they are becoming sloppy with their kills, enough to make the news. Something is going on here. We have to head back to the pack now."

Axel stepped forward. "Yes, but we can't travel tonight."

Xavier nodded and turned the television off with a hard look on his face.

I didn't like the look he had. I wasn't sure what it meant because it was the first time I'd seen him like this.

Xavier threw the television remote down and combed his hair back from his face. "I know. We'll leave at dawn." He glanced at me as if to ask for my input.

I nodded slowly.

He sat down and so did Axel.

No one moved or spoke for a while until Axel got up to get us all drinks.

I've never been someone that drinks alcohol, even socially. Suddenly, I craved it in the dim hope that it would numb my senses, if only for a while. Why? Because tomorrow would be a new day and by now, I knew it would come with new problems. This might be the last time I got to sit in comfortable silence with both Xavier and Axel for a long time to come.

This could be the last time I felt like I was out of danger and protected, especially since it was clear—a time was coming where no one would be safe.

3

RUBY

I couldn't help wondering if somewhere out there in the darkness, someone was being violently attacked and drained.

I rested my forehead against the cool glass gingerly as I closed my eyes. Unfortunately, they popped open again within seconds when an image of frightening red eyes flashed through my mind.

"Fuck."

I swallowed, but my mouth was suddenly too dry to produce any saliva. What had really happened that night? Had I died? Did our mysterious savior bring me back to life? I remembered feeling like all the life was slowly draining out of me. I hated the fact that I could still feel the fangs in my throat.

Now wasn't the time to develop PTSD. From what Axel and Xavier had told me so far, I knew a war was coming. I fisted my hand and slammed it down against my thigh. That motherfucking vamp damn near killed me!

My lips formed a thin line as I stared into the darkness

beyond the window. I was right to be afraid. Under these circumstances, it was nothing to be ashamed of. Nevertheless, I was determined to channel my fear into anger and anger into action. These creatures, these vampires, had suddenly crawled out of a hole and were on a path that would turn this world upside down. We had to find a way to stop them.

I sighed. *Who am I kidding?* No matter how angry I got, I'd never been a match for even the feeblest vampire. Though they might have been weaker than usual, if two full-grown male werewolves were almost killed, I was toast. *If I'm in this world now...*I shook my head. *No, I AM a part of this world now, and I need to be able to protect myself.*

Being mated to two werewolves would only shield me for so long. There was also no doubt in my mind that the Council, that bald prick Olcan specifically, still wanted my head– or my brain, to be more accurate. I personally wanted to know more about the woman they were talking about, their Grand Elder, myself.

If I knew her like the Enchanteds thought I did, then I wanted to understand how it could be possible that I had no conscious memory of her. Maybe she was just someone I'd encountered briefly along the way? For all I know, she could be just a customer I'd served in the diner one day.

I started chewing on my lip nervously. *Yeah, wishful thinking.* What were the chances of me knowing a Grand Elder and having a powerful supernatural barrier placed in my mind while also being a just a normal human girl who simply discovered the supernatural world by accident? Evidence of something greater going on kept stacking up, and I didn't like speculating what that could mean. There was still a slim chance this was all a strange coincidence, but I wasn't ready to bet the farm on it. In fact, it gave me a headache every time I thought about it.

I looked down at my open palm. Who was I before? Have I always been this person or was a part of me locked away? What would happen to me if I ever remembered my past?

Someone cleared their throat behind me.

I jumped around, a gasp on my lips. I blinked rapidly at Natalie.

She stood in the middle of the room, staring at me with a smile. "Hey, Redhead," she said.

I rushed to her. I hugged her tight and felt like my bones would crush with the way she hugged me back.

"Are you okay?" she asked.

"I have so much to tell you. You won't believe what happened, Natalie."

She released me and stepped back. "Try me."

"Vampires," I said. "They're real. I swear I'm not kidding…"

The smile on her face faltered. "I know."

I frowned. "How?"

Natalie turned away from me. "Olcan was called away after you guys left," she explained as she turned back around to face me.

I tried not to smile when I heard that Olcan was no longer there. Considering the fact that I'd be returning soon with the guys, Olcan was one more complication I'd just as soon avoid.

"A pack was attacked," she explained.

My brows dipped with a frown.

"They were all killed," she went on. "Women, children–every single pack member was brutally slaughtered."

I walked away from her this time, my hand over my mouth. "Jesus." I combed my hair back before my hand fell to my side. These vamps were certainly taking advantage of the element of surprise while they had it. The faster the news about their existence got out, the better people would be able to protect themselves. "We were attacked after we left the pack," I told her as I closed my eyes and pressed a finger to my temple. "One of them almost—"

Her hand came down on my shoulder as she stepped around me. She placed her hand at my neck, the spot where I'd been bitten. "I know that too," she replied sadly. "I'm so sorry."

I opened my eyes but avoided looking at her. I didn't want her to see me crying as I nodded. "You saw it?

"Yes."

"I-I can't even explain the pain. I—um," I swallowed, not wanting to think about it. "We were saved by someone. None of us saw him. Well, I kind of did before I blacked out. All I could make out for sure was his shadow, but whoever he was, he saved us and got us here."

Natalie's gaze shifted away from me.

I narrowed my eyes at her. This wasn't the response I'd expected from her. Maybe she'd seen that as well. Either way, I let it go. Something else was more important. "Did you know about vampires being alive long before I was attacked? I assume you saw the attack the night we left?"

She nodded. "Yes." She gave me a tight-lipped smile.

Why couldn't she look at me?

"Yes, I got the vision the night you left," Natalie stated.

My eyes narrowed. She was lying, I could tell. And it had been confirmed by the awkward silence that followed. If she'd known and I think she did, why hadn't she warned Xavier and me? Why hadn't she stopped us from leaving? If I'd known it would be a choice between Olcan taking me to Romania or having my throat ripped out by a vampire, I think I'd have chosen Romania. "So, Mathieu already knows about the vampires and everything? We're leaving tomorrow to head back."

Moving away from me, she answered, "Yes, he knows. The Council is trying to keep what happened to that pack under wraps, but I spoke to Reika. She told me what happened."

I shook my head. "That doesn't make sense. If these vampires are out hunting, werewolves need to know about it. Xavier and Axel got their asses handed to them, Natalie. They had no idea what the scent had meant when they picked it up until it was too late. We were all almost killed! Xavier and Axel said most werewolves have forgotten how to fight vampires. That's why the wolves need to know what's happening, while they still have a chance to prepare. Not only that, but humans are being attacked as well."

She turned to face me, a vein popping in her forehead. "I know that, Ruby! I had a friend in that pack! I understand why the Council is trying to be cautious. They fear that wolves might start to panic. In fact, I hope they do panic. Then at least they will be on guard. Otherwise, they will be sitting ducks, ripe for the hunting," She sighed. "Whoever or whatever saved you had to be supernatural, and strong at that, to have killed the vamps that attacked you guys. If we're lucky, maybe they'll show themselves soon. "

"Yeah, Axel said the same."

The side of her mouth arched at this.

I frowned. "What?"

"So, on a brighter topic," she said. "What's it like being around the two of them?"

I wasn't sure why I started blushing. "It's—fine. Okay, I guess."

"Okay? That's all you have to give me, Ruby? Really?" Her smile broke out into a grin.

I rolled my eyes and lifted my shoulders in a shrug because I had no idea what she wanted me to say. Actually, I knew what she wanted to hear, and right now things weren't like that. "Things are fine for now. The guys are still tired and weakened. They lost a lot of blood. Xavier has been quiet, and Axel is…well, Axel."

"What did you feel for Axel when you thought he was dead?"

Oh, come on, her too? Why is that so important?

"I was worried. That's all. He left his pack to come with us. If he dies, who looks after them? Who will be their alpha?"

"For someone you hate, you certainly spare a lot of thought about his people." She raised her brows, her expression otherwise blank.

"I assure you, I—" I frowned as she flickered between transparent and solid. "Natalie? Are you okay?"

She didn't reply. She just kept staring off to the side towards the room door.

I looked at the door and then her. Was she seeing or hearing something I wasn't? She flickered in and out of focus again, and I grimaced as blood began to run from her ear.

"Natalie, you're bleeding! Seriously, what's going on?" I felt panicked. I didn't think she was supposed to be bleeding like this while projecting herself to me, even if we were technically just in a dream state. What if something was wrong with her?

She turned to look at me as blood poured from her eyes. She wasn't moving, she wasn't blinking, and her face still remained as blank as a canvas.

My eyes widened as I stepped forward, my hands shaking as all the blood running from her ears and eyes began to soak through the white top she wore. "Natalie, you're freaking me out! What the fuck is happening?" My mouth clamped shut in shock.

A deep wound appeared at her neck and then her wrist. Blood now pooled around her feet.

I started pinching myself, trying to see if that would work to wake me up. If she was in my dream, she must be defenseless in reality. "Wake up!" I started yelling at both her and myself. "Wake…" I swallowed my words as a shadowy head peeked out from behind her. My heart was hammering in my chest, as shadowy claws slowly appeared and wrapped around her arm. "Who are you?" I stepped back. "What are you doing to her? How did you get in my dream?"

I dug my nails into my palm with enough force to break the skin, but I still wasn't waking up. I felt intense dread, as if a blast of evil had brushed across my soul. A scream was torn from my lips as the shadow suddenly lunged for me.

Xavier

I was fifteen when I went on my first hunt with my dad. An Echidna, a half-woman half serpent creature, was preying on humans and leaving a string of bodies in her wake.

She had struck my father with her tail, sending him flying through a window. I realized fighting her in wolf form would not stop her easily, so I changed. I waited until the other wolves created an opening, and then I buried a wooden spike through her heart.

Being a wolf and a protector means being strong. It means being smart. It means being able to protect people, especially the ones you love. I clenched my fists as I growled. Ruby almost died because I wasn't able to protect her. I hadn't been strong enough.

Full moon or not, that would never happen again.

I'd been conscious while Ruby screamed for help. With my blood rapidly leaving my body as if it was being vacuumed, I couldn't move to help her.

I'd never felt so helpless in my life. It had been agonizing to watch as the vampire attacked her. I didn't know how, but whoever saved us had also healed my broken spine. That's what that vampire had targeted. He had quickly placed himself behind me, wrapped his arms around me, and snapped my spine. No doubt, it was their way of stopping wolves from shifting.

I tapped my finger against my chest. Despite the darkness surrounding me in the room, my vision was just fine. I clenched and unclenched my hand, testing my strength.

Although there'd be no way in hell we'd travel while it was still dark, I needed to be at full strength when we traveled back to the pack tomorrow.

Also, there wouldn't be a full moon tomorrow night. At least I'd be able to shift if needed.

The sooner we got back to the pack, the faster Axel could retrieve the book to help us defeat those bloodsuckers.

I noticed Ruby and Axel had seemed unusually chatty with each other. Yes, I'm bothered by that. I obviously know he is her mate. I also know there must be a part of her that cared about him, even if she didn't show it. She proved that the night we were attacked.

Now that I knew he was on our side, I didn't want to rip his throat out as much. Doing so would hurt her emotionally more than before. I held my hand to my forehead and wished desperately for some pain meds. I didn't get headaches often, but this shit show was getting to me. Not only did we have the Council and vampires to contend with on top of an unexplainable three-way mate bond, but we still didn't know what might lurk behind that barrier in Ruby's mind.

A bloodcurdling scream echoed through the house—Ruby's scream. I bolted out of bed. Her bedroom was right across from mine, so I kicked the door open and rushed in. My eyes scanned the room quickly, but I saw no one.

Ruby was still in bed, her arms and legs thrashing around as she screamed.

I realized she must be dreaming, so I immediately rushed to her. "Ruby, wake up. Wake up, baby. It's just a dream."

She kept screaming, tears flowing from her closed eyes.

Axel rushed into the room. "What's going on?" His eyes

were that of his wolf, black pits, while his claws were out and ready to strike.

"She's having a nightmare," I told him. I moved back as one of her legs came close to hitting me. Each time I attempted to touch her, she started to howl louder and push me away.

"What the fuck kind of nightmare is she having?" Axel hissed as he retracted his claws and rushed over to the bed. "Ruby." He cupped her cheek gently.

I couldn't help sinking my teeth into my tongue as he touched her.

"Ruby, wake up! Can you hear me?"

More tears began to flow from her eyes.

He held her arm to stop her flailing, but staggered back when her other hand thrust outward and punched him right in the face.

She bolted upright, her eyes wide as she looked around the room frantically. Finally, she looked at me and then at Axel, who held his busted nose. She began wiping at her eyes.

"Ruby?" I prompted.

She climbed out of bed and walked away, her shoulders rising and falling rapidly with her heavy breathing. "I'm okay," she reassured us, her back still turned. "I-I was talking to Natalie. Olcan left because vampires attacked a pack and killed everyone."

"Fuck!" Axel exclaimed as he stepped up beside me. "When? What pack?"

"I don't know," she replied. "We were talking when—when something happened." She turned around to face us, her eyes red-rimmed and puffy from crying. "She started bleeding out of her ears and eyes, and then her neck and wrist. It was like she was being attacked."

I closed my eyes for a second before reopening them, my thoughts already running rampant with negativity. I took a deep breath and reminded myself that I needed to think positively. After all, Natalie could have appeared like that to Ruby for any reason. Then again, this had never happened before to my knowledge, and Natalie had done plenty of mind links in the past.

"If Olcan's not there, we can call," Axel suggested. "We can check if something actually happened."

I nodded.

Ruby just hung her head as she pinched the bridge of her nose. "Something was behind her, a shadow, or something." She looked up at us, her eyes full of tears. "It attacked me."

"I'm going for the house phone. We'll call and check on them," Axel declared.

He turned to leave the room when Ruby stopped him. "There's something I didn't tell you," she disclosed to me before glancing over at Axel. "Something I saw in the mind link with Natalie and Reika." She swallowed. "The shadows I saw."

Axel squinted his eyes in confusion. "Shadows? What kind of shadows?"

Heading over to the bed, she sat down. "During the mind link, I saw a vision or maybe a memory. I was in a town or city. People were running and screaming and these shadows were chasing after them. The mind link started to break when one of the shadows attacked a woman." She closed her eyes and combed her hair out of her face. "I saw those same shadows again in the pack house, the night we left. At first, I just thought I was just seeing things. However, this is now the third time I've seen them, both in my mind and in reality.

"Why didn't you tell me about this sooner?" I asked her. "Is that why I caught you running that night?"

Ruby nodded. "Yes. I didn't say anything, Xavier, because with everything else going on and our lives in jeopardy, it didn't seem very important. I'm telling you both now. So, what do you think it means?"

Axel shrugged. "Ghosts are really the only possibility for what you saw in the house because werewolves can't smell them. Any other supernatural would have been detectable by their scent."

"Do you think it's all in my head?" she asked tentatively and paused before shaking her head definitively. "No. No, I know something's wrong. Something's not right, Axel." She placed her face in her hands. "I can feel it. Something's not right. Why is all of this happening?"

I looked over at Axel.

He stared at Ruby with concern.

I sank down to my knees in front of her and attempted to gently pry her hands away from her face. I wasn't surprised she felt panicked. She'd been through so much already and there seemed to be no end in sight.

On top of everything, now she had to live with the memory of what that vampire had done to her. She'd become a part of this world now, with so much going on around her, so many things she wasn't used to. There were creatures in my world that would scare anyone to death, and she had already come face to face with one. She was a strong woman, incredibly strong, but too much was being dumped into her lap far too quickly.

I was used to the chaos of my world. She wasn't…not yet anyway.

"Hey, look at me, hey." She finally did and I gently held her chin. "Axel is going to call the house to check on Natalie and the others. As for the shadows, we'll figure it all out when we get back to the pack. Okay?"

Ruby kept breathing rapidly. "We need to find a witch. I want to know what's inside my head. I want to know what was done to me." She placed her hand against her chest, "Something is wrong, Xavier. I can feel it."

Axel frowned deeply, his forehead furrowed to the point that his brows were almost touching.

As he stepped forward, Ruby looked up at him and sniffled.

To my surprise, his hard expression softened as he gazed down at her.

"Once we get you back to Xavier's pack," he explained in a soft voice. " I'll contact the witch that made the scent dampening potions for me. I'll see if she can help. If she can't, I'll have her find someone who can. The warlock here isn't strong enough when it comes to mind links. It's not his specialty. Asking him to help might hurt you both." I didn't miss the way his hand twitched before he stepped back. The indifferent mask he typically wore returned. "Try and get some sleep. We're leaving at daybreak."

4

RUBY

*W*e headed out at daybreak in accordance with the plan and drove throughout the day.

Xavier and Axel repeatedly tried calling Natalie, but the call kept going to voicemail. It didn't fill me with confidence that she was all right. I was terrified that we might return to find a house filled with dead wolves.

We barely spoke to each other. I assumed Xavier and Axel were lost in their own thoughts, just like I was.

At around 5 pm, we started looking for a motel to avoid traveling through the night. Axel took his own room, while Xavier and I shared one.

We might have wished we could continue to travel at night, but that shit wasn't going to happen. Not while we still knew so little about the bloodsuckers. At least Xavier and Axel now knew their scent, but what good would that do if we were attacked again? Thankfully, it wasn't a full moon, so the guys were at full strength, but we were taking nothing for granted. What if there were more than two vampires? Xavier and Axel would be outnumbered, and I wouldn't stand a chance.

Xavier and my room contained twin beds, a television so small, even I could've picked it up and thrown it without effort, and a mini-fridge. I could see Xavier in my peripheral vision on the next bed over as I laid on my back on the incredibly uncomfortable bed, a bedspring digging into me, causing me to shift every three seconds.

He had his hands behind his head as he stared up at the ceiling. I sighed and scooted closer to the edge of the bed to get some relief.

"Are you okay?" he asked as he turned onto his side to face me.

I nodded.

"The shadow that you saw behind Natalie–was it more like a person that was blurry or a plain black shadow?"

"A plain black shadow," I replied as I turned onto my side to face him. "Why?"

"I'm just curious. You saw that first during the mind link and you've been seeing shadows ever since. That has to mean something."

I rolled onto my back. "I know. I feel like it does too. It has to." I rested my arm on my forehead. "There is so much going on, so much to think about. I don't have a headache, but this tension in my head's driving me nuts."

"I know what you mean. We'll get the answers we need soon enough. It won't do you any good trying to speculate or try to find answers where there are none."

I snorted. "That's easier said than done." I rolled back onto my side, the lamp sitting between our beds illuminating his face and making his eyes shine. "Do you think they're okay?"

He nodded, knowing whom I was speaking of. "She's fine. They're okay. We'll leave early in the morning again, and it'll be just a few more hours before we get there." He propped himself up on his elbow. "They're all right."

I could hear it in his voice—he was trying to convince himself of that as well. I bit down on my lip. I hadn't considered the fact that although Natalie was my friend, she was also his cousin—his family. They were all his family. Of course, he would be worried since none of their calls had been returned. "I'm hungry," I muttered softly to myself.

Sitting up, he swung his legs off the bed.

"Where are you going?"

He bent down to put his shoes on before getting up. "I'm hungry as well. I'll go get some snacks from the vending machine in the lobby, okay?"

I nodded and watched him leave before I turned the lamp off. Sometimes lying in the dark offered some comfort. With a bit of light coming in through the window by the door, I could tell if anyone walked by the door.

I was becoming paranoid, but after everything that had happened, I thought I had a right to be. Hence, the knife hidden safely under my pillow.

I wasn't sure when I dozed off, but a rattling sound in the room woke me up. Trapped in the state between awake and asleep, I rolled onto my side to face the door as I rubbed at my eyes. "Xavier?"

When I got no response, I opened my sleep-crusted eyes and spotted someone standing in the corner of the room. I blinked rapidly, my heart skipping a beat as I realized it wasn't Xavier. I jumped up and turned the lamp on before reaching under the pillow for the knife.

When I looked back, I could just make out the form of a man. It did not look like a solid person but instead, it appeared smoky and indistinct. It was seeping into the walls. My eyes bulged as a scream rose to my mouth. I jumped out of bed, tripped, and fell, my eyes still on the smoky form that was almost gone. I got up and rushed to the door. When I opened the door, I almost ran directly into a tall form with a pair of bright eyes staring down at me. Blinded by fear and pumped up on adrenaline, my fist acted on its own.

Luckily, Axel was quick to grab my hand. "Ruby, what the hell? Why are you screaming?" He focused on the room and moved past me to get into the room.

I pushed him out and slammed the door behind me. "There's someone in the room, *was* someone in the room. It was a shadow." I squeezed my eyes shut. "No, not a shadow. There was someone there, but he turned into smoke." I opened my eyes. I didn't like the way he was looking at me. "He turned into fucking smoke! You have to believe me!"

He reached out to me and held my shoulder. "Hey, I believe you. Come on." He took my hand.

As we walked, I couldn't stop looking around. "Someone is watching me, Axel. Something's wrong here."

"Nothing is wrong with you," he said as he opened his room door and let me in. "Where is Xavier?"

"He went to get food. Do you think he's okay?"

He didn't answer as he went to his window and peeked outside. "He's fine, see?" Since the lobby was a straight shot across from his room, he could see Xavier through the glass door standing at the counter.

I leaned forward to confirm Xavier's wellbeing then breathed a sigh of relief that only calmed me for a second. I hadn't imagined it—I was sure of it. Someone had been watching me sleep.

"There wasn't a scent in the room other than yours and Xavier's," he said as he sat down on the bed. "I guess they could have masked their scent, though."

I plopped down beside him and looked over at him, his statement not helping to calm me down at all. "The person is still here, Axel. All he did was fade into the wall. He's still here. We can't stay here." I sighed as I glanced down at my feet. In my panic, I had run out of my room without putting shoes on.

I didn't know how he could be so calm. If he believed me, there was no way he'd be this calm.

"We can't leave. If someone was watching you, they had a lot of time to hurt you, if that was their intention." He walked over to his backpack where it sat on a chair across the room. He returned with a pair of socks in hand and handed them to me. "They're clean. Put them on."

I stared at the socks but made no move to take them. I just kept seeing the image of black smoke in the shape of a man.

He sighed and bent down. "We can't leave tonight. It's not wise for us to travel at night."

I broke out of my trance when his warm hand lifted my leg. I watched as he slid the socks onto my feet one at a time and slowly, very slowly. My cheeks began to heat, and I rubbed my hands against them. I dropped my hands as he looked up at me. My heart skipped a beat as his hazel eyes bored into mine.

His hand was still on my foot, but the moment lasted for just a second as he looked away and stood up. "No one will get to you," he declared confidently as he walked back over to his bag. "I'll make sure of it." He zipped the bag closed and turned to face me, his long hair hanging over his back and shoulders. "I'll protect you, Ruby. You know that, don't you?"

The promise in his voice was somehow enough to make me calm down. "Yes," I answered slowly. "You know, you're not a complete dick."

The lip arched. "You caught me in a good mood. Give me some time."

I rolled my eyes.

He chuckled as he moved to sit beside me once more.

"Sorry about punching you in the face last night."

Axel touched his nose before leaning his head back on his hands. "No worries. You pack a punch, but your hands are still too small to do too much damage."

I punched him in the side as hard as I could.

He yelped and sat up.

"You were saying?" I stated.

"Damn, did you really have to do that?" He chuckled. "This is abuse."

I couldn't help but giggle as I leaned a little closer to him. "I'm learning from the best." I pulled away as I continued to laugh.

Suddenly, his laughter died away. His expression changed.

My laughter halted. "What?"

His jaws clenched. "I'm sorry for what I did to you." He rubbed his cheek as he looked away. "The dungeon. All of it."

I raised a brow in shock.

Before I could say anything, the room door opened and Xavier walked in. "What's going on?"

Axel got up and headed for the bathroom. "Someone was in her room."

"What?" Xavier asked as he dropped the bag in his hand. "Who? Where are they?"

"They seeped into the wall," Axel yelled from the bathroom before reappearing, his hair now in a bun. "Whoever or whatever it was had been watching her sleep."

Xavier looked towards the door and then back at me. "Shit. I had heard a scream but that moron in the lobby was watching a horror movie. It was so loud, I thought the scream came from it."

Axel picked up his bag and placed it on the floor before sitting down. "There was no scent in the room. None other than the usual nasties you pick up at a motel, anyways. It must have been masked, and we can't exactly knock on every door to check if there is a supernatural inside."

Xavier sighed and picked up the bag he had dropped. He removed two Twinkies and threw one to Axel before giving the bag to me. "You should eat something now. Axel and I will stay up. We'll take turns to watch if this shadow person returns."

I looked from one man to the other. Right now, at this moment, the curse of being mated to both of them felt like a blessing. I took the bag from Xavier and scooted up to the headboard. "I don't think I can sleep now," I admitted as I ripped into a Doritos bag.

"That's fine. You'll fall asleep eventually," Axel replied as he slid down in the chair somewhat and glanced at Xavier. "You're on the first watch."

Xavier threw him a nasty look and sat on the bed beside me. I offered him some of my Doritos but he declined. "Eat. You need it more than I do. Was this one of the shadows like before?"

I shook my head. "No. Those shadows were exactly that, solid shadows. This one was more smoke-like."

He said nothing after that but remained by my side.

Even though I'd said I wouldn't be able to sleep, knowing they were both watching over me had me drifting off pretty soon.

Axel

Since I'd taken the last watch until early this morning, Xavier drove us back to the pack. The moment we arrived, I could tell something was off. I noticed Xavier looked wary as well.

Ruby took off running towards the house as soon as the car came to a stop. She ignored me telling her to slow down as she started screaming Natalie's name.

Footsteps approaching us rapidly caught my ear and Natalie appeared, her white hair piled high on her head.

Ruby pulled her into a hug. "Where the fuck is your phone? We've been calling you and Mathieu. Neither of you answered."

"Um, I have no idea where it is, to be honest," Natalie replied. "So much has been happening around here."

"Like what?" Xavier asked as he pulled her into a hug.

"What happened the other night when you mind-linked me?" Ruby added.

Natalie held her hands up. "Okay seriously, what's going on? Come on, I'll fix you guys something to eat. You all look like shit."

Ruby sighed as she followed Natalie into the kitchen.

I lingered in the back while I leaned on the edge of the door. The house seemed quiet, more than usual.

"You started flickering between looking transparent and normal. Then you started bleeding..." Ruby waved her hand over Natalie's body. "...Out of everywhere." She slid onto a stool around the island. "There was a shadow behind you. It appeared after you started bleeding, and then it attacked me. I thought maybe you were hurt, that you were being attacked here."

Natalie looked thoughtful for a moment. She moved a few strands of stray hair away from her face. "No. Our connection broke. I figured you were waking up or something. Nothing like that happened here last night."

"Where is everyone?" I asked. "It's quiet here, more than usual."

"Yeah, I noticed that too. Where's dad?" Xavier asked.

Natalie didn't give an answer as she walked over to the fridge and began removing eggs, bacon, and everything she needed to make a meal.

Of course, I wasn't planning on sticking around to have a feast, I had my pack to check on. All I wanted was to make sure Ruby made it back safe.

"He took the pack to a secret location," Natalie replied as she braced herself on the island.

Xavier frowned.

"He's been moving the pack slowly. After that entire pack was killed, vampires tried to kill the Council member from Europe." She poured three glasses of orange juice for Xavier and Ruby but I declined. "All the Council members are on lockdown right now. They're targeting wolves first, and it's a smart move on their part. However, other supernaturals are being attacked as well."

"So, it's getting out there that they're real then?" Ruby asked.

Natalie nodded. "Yes. Everyone is on high alert."

I scratched my chin and walked further into the kitchen. "Why are they attacking now? They've been living in secret for longer than anyone remembers. Now all of a sudden, they're attacking Council members. Where have they been all this time?"

Natalie sipped from the glass she offered me and shrugged. "I have no idea and right now, we can't worry about that. What about your pack?"

"I sent a message to my beta before we left to head back here," I told her.

Nodding as she listened, she cracked eggs to whisk together.

I went on, "It's only a matter of time before the humans start to connect the dots. They are draining people like they're Gatorades at half-time. Worse yet, they're being sloppy about it. They're not even bothering to hide their kills anymore."

Natalie snorted. "Well, at least now, there is something else on the news other than humans murdering each other. This world is already shit for us, and now we have vampires to worry about."

"They're like any other paranormal that plagues humans and risks the exposure of the entire supernatural community. They'll be dealt with accordingly," Xavier said in a low voice before slamming his fist down on the island. "But for all the training we've done over the years, nothing has prepared us for this. It snapped my spine like a toothpick."

Natalie's face dropped. "What?"

"One of the vampires that attacked us," he told her. "It broke my back. I think if you do some research on how that pack was all murdered, there'll be a lot of dead wolves with snapped spines. Fighting them in wolf form will mean we'll be at full strength, strong enough to rip them to shreds, but at higher risk of one climbing onto our back."

I frowned, as he hadn't told me this. "The one that attacked me didn't do that. It went straight for my chest. My heart maybe?"

Xavier nodded. "They try to not prolong a fight with a wolf. They try to make their first strike...the last. Their scent is their greatest disadvantage. If they learn to mask that, we'll be screwed. I think if they haven't figured out how to over the years they've been in hiding, they can't."

"That's a start then, right?" Ruby asked. "Having an idea of how they'll attack. At least we know that much and can pass it on to other packs. What about sunlight and being staked through the heart? Do you guys think all of that will actually kill them?"

"Sunlight, yes," I replied. "Being staked, no, that's bullshit. They're already dead, so they don't have a beating heart. Go for the head. They also heal quickly, so decapitating them has to be done quickly. You can also completely dismember them. At least that's what I think I saw in that book. It's been years." I rubbed my hands together as I tried to picture the book and everything I had seen within it. "Wolves and a handful of other supernaturals are strong and fast enough to fight them and win. Plus, we smell them so easily." I looked at Xavier. "Thinking about vampire-fighting style now, I think my pack has been incorporating techniques in our training to fight them." I gave him a smug grin. Although I knew now wasn't the time to be petty, there was no way I could let the opportunity pass.

His eyes lowered as his jaws clenched.

I turned away. "I'm going back to my pack. I'll secure their safety and return with the book."

I glanced at Ruby over my shoulder, her green eyes pierced into mine. I looked away without saying anything. It was becoming increasingly difficult for me to look her in the eyes without feeling things I didn't want to. I figured being away from her for a few hours might do me some good.

"Hey," Xavier called behind me.

I got to the front door and turned around to face him. "Yeah?" The time we'd spent together had left us less hostile towards each other, but I still didn't like the guy. As much as I'd never admit it to anyone, that's partly because of how close he was to Ruby. They deserved each other, as they were true mates. She and I were just an accident made by the goddess.

Even so, I still cared for her…I still dreamt about her.

"Why are you doing this?" Xavier asked. "Helping Ruby and I and willing to pass on useful information so easily."

I inhaled as I buried my hands in my pockets. I looked past him to the direction of the kitchen as Ruby's laughter met my ears. I rarely heard her laugh, but when I did, I tried to imprint it to my memory. "What's going on right now is bigger than land and power. Some things are more important." I cleared my throat as my eyes drifted back to him while Ruby and Natalie began to whisper. "Besides, if we don't work together and these leeches take over, everything will be theirs. That's all there is to it."

I turned away without another word and closed the door silently behind me.

5

RUBY

*I*t felt weird being back in this house. I sat up in bed staring before rising and heading to the window. There has always been something calming about watching the world outside one's window. Whether it is night or day, I can sit at a window and feel a heavy weight lifted off my shoulders.

After Axel left, I chatted with Natalie for a while before relaxing in a luxuriously long shower and going to sleep. I felt exhausted and frankly still on edge after seeing that shadow person watching me. I was trying not to think about the fact that it might have followed us here. I had slept during the day to be awake during the night.

I woke up after 5 pm and found the house empty. I'd been in my room since. Knowing only a few wolves were patrolling the forest, I just wanted to be in my room where I felt at least somewhat safe.

The towering trees outside my window weren't offering me the calm I had hoped for. The forest here was thicker than where Axel's safe house was. I was becoming more uneasy the longer I stared out the window. I felt like within those trees...something was staring back at me.

I drew the curtain and turned away.

Natalie walked into the room at that moment. "Hey," she said as she plopped down on my bed.

"Hey." I sat beside her. "I wish we didn't have to stay here for the night. I know Mathieu will be back in the morning to take us to where everyone else is, but couldn't we have gone into the city, rented somewhere for the night?" I turned to face her. "I mean, there's no one here. If we're attacked, we'll surely die."

She placed her hand over mine and gave me a reassuring smile. "There are several warrior wolves in the forest. We aren't alone. I slept here last night alone and I was perfectly fine."

I'd been trying hard not to panic as she tried to reassure me. I sighed. "It's not just the vampires I'm afraid of. Someone is watching me, Natalie. That shadow guy or whatever that thing was in my room the other night at the motel freaked me out."

"I'd be freaked out too, so I understand."

"I feel uncomfortable being here with everything that occurred before I left. I saw the shadows here as well, so staying right now doesn't exactly make me feel safe."

Frowning, she asked, "You saw shadows here in the house?"

I nodded and told her about what I'd seen during our mind link.

She looked confused the more I spoke. Eventually, she stood up and started pacing.

"I didn't say anything because there wasn't any time to," I added.

She nodded, looking perplexed. "No, no, I get it. I understand why you said nothing. I'm wondering why I didn't see that during the mind link. I doubt Reika saw it either. I think she would have told me if she had."

"You trust her?" I asked her.

Again, she nodded. "I do. She helped me out that night when you guys left, and she's been filling me in on what's been going on with the Council since. She can be trusted. Xavier was telling me earlier about everything that happened with the vampires that attacked you guys." She sat down again.

I let out a sigh. I closed my eyes and bit down on my lip for a second as the vivid memory of terrifying red eyes entered my mind unbidden. "I thought I was going to die," I said in a low voice. "He was tearing into me, Natalie. Have you ever seen a dog bite down on something and shake it? That's what…" I closed my eyes for a moment as my body tensed up. The memory was too painful. "It was the most horrible thing I've ever experienced in my life. I could feel my blood rushing to my neck."

She moved my hair over my shoulder. "I'm sorry you had to go through that. Now you know what these creatures are like, the monsters that they are. All three of you do. As for whoever saved you guys…" She puckered her lips. "I don't know. Either that person was following you guys, following the vampires, or was just at the right place at the right time."

"How did he know where to take us, though?"

"I don't know." She shrugged. "Xavier told me you were all in pretty bad shape. If he or she healed all three of you, they must have been strong. If I had to guess, I would say the person had to be a powerful witch or warlock, or possibly even a demon. Whomever it was, they're an ally if they saved you all. All-powerful allies like that will be needed in the fight to come." Grasping my shoulders, she turned me to face her.

"What are you doing?" I asked.

Moving my hair back on my other shoulder, she hovered her hand over the area where I had been bitten. She closed her eyes for a moment. When they reopened, they were as white as clouds. "There are traces of magic on you. It definitely was a witch or something, but it's fading."

"I didn't say this to the guys," I whispered. "But I think that shadow in my room was the person who saved us. I hadn't realized that might be the case until I woke up the next morning."

Pulling her hand away, she pursed her lips as her white eyes faded back to blue. "That could be true, yes."

"Fight to come?" I repeated. I felt like Natalie knew more than she was letting on. "You said there is a fight to come. How do you know that? Have you had a vision?"

"No, it's just clear if the vampires aren't stopped soon, things will get out of hand."

"Who's going to stop them? The Council members are focusing on their own safety right now."

Despite how crappy the human government could be, I was certain that when, not if, they found out about vampires, they'd use everything in their power to fight back and protect their people. The werewolf Council wanted to hide the existence of vampires even as the bloodsuckers were slaughtering packs one by one.

Natalie smoothed my brows down with a finger. "Our pack and the ones that are willing to fight will have to come together. We have to start hunting the vampires. We will need everyone's help."

"No," I said. "I've faced one of those monsters already, Natalie. I saw his eyes, and now I can't stop seeing them. I can't face another one of them. I don't have the strength you and the other wolves have, so count me out. When that fight starts, I'll be locked in a room surrounded by a circle of guns. That's all I can do to protect myself."

She didn't say anything for a while.

I didn't care how selfish it sounded. Unlike the Council members, who had the power to help and refused, I couldn't help even if I wanted to. If Axel and Xavier had to watch over me at all times, it distracted them and put them at greater risk. Axel had his pack to look after and Xavier needed to help his father to protect their people.

"I saw the way Axel looked at you before he left," she whispered. "Are you two becoming closer?"

I folded my lips in contemplation. I thought of Axel's apology for how he had treated me in the beginning and shrugged. "We're not close, but at least we're civil. He left with us, putting himself in danger and leaving his pack without a real leader. He...um, he apologized for everything."

A smile spread across her lips

I rolled my eyes. "Stop smiling like that. All he did was apologize to me. I would say he owed me at least that much." Despite the truth of my words, I couldn't stop the flutter of butterfly wings in my belly. Axel had seemed different, kinder. It was only a sprinkle of kindness in an otherwise hostile personality made up of 95% asshole. But because of this fact, whenever he said something sweet or did something kind, I knew it was real.

Natalie stayed with me for a while as we talked about some of her past relationships and my failed ones. I cherished the momentary distraction from what was happening around us. Even if it was only for a little while, it was almost like we were just two normal college girls gossiping about boys and our experiences. Not vampires and a war neither of us can fight.

Natalie

I had experienced the vision of Ruby being attacked as if I had been Ruby herself. While I hadn't experienced her pain, I had felt her intense fear as she looked into the petrifying blood-red eyes of that vampire.

As I laid in bed unable to sleep, it felt like I could see those spine-chilling red eyes looking down at me from the ceiling. I closed my eyes as they began to tear up. I'd turned into a liar ever since I got my new powers. While I was doing this for good reasons...it didn't stop how horrible I felt. I couldn't tell Ruby I had seen her attack long before it had happened. How would I explain to her that it had been my job to lead her to it? I wasn't told why, but I could only assume there were things I didn't know, things I couldn't explain.

I was merely a servant.

What good could come from her being attacked by a

vampire? I wasn't sure of the answer. The only thing I did feel sure of was that her being bitten was completely unavoidable. If it hadn't happened that night, it would have happened another night and the outcome could have been even worse. Either way, she had to see what vampires were like for herself—they all needed to see it.

The role Xavier, Axel, and Ruby were going to play in the future depended on their hatred for vampires. What better way of solidifying that hatred than by having a true score to settle? That's why I thought she needed to be bitten. The vampires that attacked them had been killed—that part I didn't see. I hadn't known how they would be saved, just that they would be. Even though those vampires were killed, Axel, Xavier, and Ruby would hold this newfound hatred close to them.

Vampires were fueled by hunger and rage. To beat them… it had to be matched.

I said nothing to Ruby when she admitted to being scared because I was terrified too. As for the shadows she was seeing and whoever was following her, I knew nothing about those. I wasn't sure how I felt about being kept in the dark about some of this.

Sensing something, I frowned as I looked over at my door. I swallowed as a metallic taste suddenly filled in my mouth. I bolted upright out of bed and ran to the bathroom where I flipped on my light. I stuck my tongue out in front of the mirror, and crimson droplets rolled off my tongue into the white basin of the sink below. My tongue was dripping with blood.

"Something's very wrong."

I rushed out of the room in my nightclothes, leaving my

shoes behind. I wasn't sure exactly what was happening, but death was coming, I could feel it. I rushed to Ruby's room and found her fast asleep. I breathed a sigh of relief, but the foreboding feeling did not fade or even lessen.

I closed her room door and headed back to my own room, unsure of what to do next. All of a sudden, a piercing howl from outside pierced the air. It sounded like a wolf in pain, and the metallic taste of blood permeated my mouth again. My gut twisted as I turned and headed for the stairs.

As I sprinted down the stairs, the front door flew open wildly.

Axel rushed in. He dropped a bulky bag and rubbed his arm as if it were sore from the weight.

I looked behind me to the second floor where Xavier appeared. Without hesitation, he threw himself over the railing and fell to the first floor, righting himself quickly. I took the rest of the stairs two at a time.

"What's going on?" he asked Axel, who was still panting.

Axel turned away to hastily close the door behind himself. "Where is Ruby?"

"Sleeping," I answered. "What's going on? I heard a wolf's howl, and we didn't expect you back tonight," I added. "Did something hap—" I coughed as blood began to pour from my lips. Another penetrating howl rang through the night. I could smell it then, a rancid smell.

Xavier grabbed my shoulder and our eyes met as we heard another wolf's cry.

"No," I said as I wiped at my mouth.

"What the fuck is going on right now?" Xavier asked.

I swallowed as I turned to him slowly and shook my head. "Can't you smell that?"

"I can't smell it. They're too far away. How can you?" Axel asked me.

"I'm an Enchanted, remember?" I turned to Xavier, whose confusion was slowly fading from his face as he realized what was happening. I nodded as he released my shoulder. "They're coming. The vampires are coming, Xavier. We have to get Ruby—now!"

6

RUBY

"*A*re you hearing me?"

It took a moment for me to realize Natalie was speaking to me. I looked down at the backpack she was handing to me and nodded before taking it. "I'm hearing you."

She looked at me strangely for a moment. "We need to move quickly Ruby. I was saying there are tunnels under the house for situations like this. We'll be using them." She bent down to zip up her backpack.

"Yeah, I heard you," I replied.

Axel knelt next to the hefty bag filled with weapons that he arrived with. The book he had told us about laid beside it.

The chocolate brown leather covered book with it's aged brown pages appeared much bigger than I'd originally expected. If I were to hold it up, it would cover almost my entire chest. It was titled "The History of the Damned", and I wondered what other paranormal creatures I might find in there.

"We need to move," Axel said as he placed three guns and

several clips in his backpack while Xavier did the same. "My beta relocated the majority of the pack, and I sent the rest packing. I was almost out the door when they attacked. I made it to my car and bolted as fast as I could. I figured they'd either be coming here next or another group was already on their way." He stood up and swung his bag over his shoulder. He held his hand up for silence and tilted his head somewhat. His eyes turned black as he called on his wolf, and I watched as the tip of his ears began to elongate.

His brows twitched for a moment and then stopped. "I can't tell how many of them there are, but they're getting closer. They're moving quietly but swiftly. The branches and twigs they don't miss are giving them away." He glanced over at Xavier. "You can smell them now, right?" Axel's ears returned to normal as his black eyes reverted to hazel.

Xavier nodded.

I swallowed despite how dry my mouth was. *They're coming.* Those monsters are coming here. I inhaled deeply but couldn't smell anything.

I threw my bag onto my back and remained to the side while they did their thing. I knew I would only get in the way.

Xavier picked up a dagger and turned it over in his hand before putting it back in the bag and picking up a larger knife instead. "I can't leave my men out there. They're being picked off one by one."

"If you go out there now, you'll just die with them," Natalie said. "We warned the men when you got here about what to expect. You don't know that they won't survive."

Xavier's jaw clenched.

"Those wolves are all dead," Axel suddenly said.

Xavier growled now.

Leave it up to Axel to make a bad situation worse. "Three of my best trained men were killed when they broke into my house, and as I said, my pack has already been incorporating some techniques that are *supposed* to work on them. Maybe some of your men will survive, but you going out there right now in a vain attempt to protect them is foolish."

Xavier's face was twisted with rage, but he recognized the wisdom in Axel's words.

I was thankful that Xavier saw reason since I feared what would happen to him if he went out there with his men. I also hated the idea that the tunnels we would have to take would eventually lead us outside.

Why the fuck do we have to go outside?

I closed my eyes and inhaled deeply. I called on my anger as I tried to push my terror deep down within myself. One of those leeches almost sucked me dry like a Slurpee. We might be running for our lives, but I damn sure wouldn't be running while pissing myself with fear. I had no intention of becoming some bloodsucking asshole's midnight snack.

I opened my eyes and stepped forward. Bending down, I searched through the weapons bag for anything that I could use to protect myself. I found two silver daggers that were long and pointy. They looked almost like ice picks. I secured one dagger up the long sleeve top I wore under my jacket, comforted by the feeling of the cool steel against my skin. I shoved the other into my waist. I grabbed the knife-like dagger Xavier had discarded and shoved it into the side of my boot.

"Someone is ready for war, I see," Axel remarked.

I gazed up at him.

He stared at me with a smirk on his lips.

I narrowed my eyes at him, and he snorted and turned away.

I looked over at Xavier as he approached me and cupped my cheeks. "I want you to stay by my side. Do you understand? When I say run, Ruby, I want you to run."

An agonized howl that sounded like it was just outside the house chilled the blood in my veins.

Xavier's eyes turned black.

My heart started pounding against my rib cage.

Xavier and Axel looked to the ceiling at the same time, and Natalie soon did the same.

I wondered what the hell they were all doing. "What's wrong?"

"Shh," Axel hissed.

I looked at Xavier, and he placed a finger to his lips. I swallowed, the sound of my heartbeat hammering in my ears as he held his hand out to me.

They're in the house!

Swiftly, I placed my hand in his.

Natalie picked up the book on the ground.

I frowned with puzzlement as Xavier removed his bag from his back. He put it on in his front to cover his chest.

He turned his back to me while bending down somewhat. He looked at me over his shoulder and patted his back softly.

After I climbed onto his back, Natalie led us out of the kitchen and past the lobby down a hallway to the right. I couldn't hear their footsteps despite how quickly they were walking. I knew if I'd been walking alongside them, the squeak of my shoes would've given us away.

Natalie led the way in front. Xavier and I were the middle

while Axel pulled up the rear. I tightened my hold around Xavier's neck, and he reached up to run a hand down the side of my face.

All three of them came to an abrupt stop.

I thought maybe we had come to a secret door in the wall or something, but then an odd odor had my nose crinkling with disgust.

My eyes widened with realization as I looked behind us.

Xavier and Axel turned around at the same time.

A vampire stood behind us, a woman with the sides of her head shaved and the rest of her hair in a ponytail. She hissed at us, baring her long fangs as her clawed fingers wiggled.

With the lights above us, I could clearly see the black veins running up her throat to stop just under her bottom lip. I hadn't noticed those veins on the vampire that attacked me, but it had been really dark at the time.

Her eyes were as red as the vampire's that attacked me. She smiled, her mouth stretching wide.

My heart began to beat even faster, as Xavier bent down for me to slide off his back. I held onto his shirt as he stepped forward, but he quickly freed himself from my grasp. He touched Axel's shoulder and nodded his head toward my direction.

Axel stepped to my side.

My eyes widened as Xavier's shoulder suddenly snapped.

"No," I said under my breath as I stepped forward.

Axel grabbed my arm.

"No!" I said lower.

Xavier's back hunched and his shirt began to rip as he started to shift.

I removed the dagger from under my sleeve, and Axel began pulling on my arm.

We can't leave him behind. There's no way in hell I'll leave him behind. Human or not, I won't run!

The vampire hissed and Xavier's deep gravelly growl echoed through the house. "Remember what I said, Ruby." His voice was contorted, a blend of the human Xavier and his wolf. He groaned as his right knee snapped. "Run!"

Axel's hold on me tightened, and I had no choice but to run as he pulled me. Xavier charged forward, and I saw a glimpse of dark brown fur appear through the torn skin on his back. We rounded a corner, our legs pumping to propel us forward.

Tears were streaming down my face as I listened to Xavier's deep howls and growls. Axel released my hand so I could wipe my tears as Natalie kicked the library door open. I ran inside after her. Then I stepped away from both of them, my hands on my head as they barricaded the door. "We can't leave him," I said under my voice before turning to face them. "We can't leave him! He can't fight them alone!"

Natalie shoved the book over to Axel as she walked over to a wall with a large painting of a ship being wrecked at sea.

I felt like this house was that ship.

She ran her hand against the side of the painting and then pulled. The painting swung away from the wall like a door. The wall behind it appeared flat and plain. Natalie pressed her hand against the surface. A small square sank in to release a previously invisible door.

I turned to Axel. "We can't leave him, Axel. You said it yourself, we don't know how many of them are out there. He can't fight them all!" It sounded like the house was being ripped apart. Each time I heard Xavier's thundering howls, the blood chilled in my veins.

"Please, Axel!"

He walked over to me and held my face gently as I held onto his hand. "I know," he replied and then released my face to hold my elbow. He pulled me to the open door where Natalie was waiting. I looked behind her at the dark passage before turning back to him. "Axel?"

He handed the book back to Natalie. "Go, both of you. I'll go back and help Xavier, but I need the two of you to leave. Understood? Don't wait for us."

Despite being petrified of leaving Xavier to fight alone, deserting Axel as well only made me feel worse. I didn't want to lose either of them, and I doubted whoever saved us before was hanging out somewhere around the house just waiting to help us again. I had to hold onto what tiny comfort I was getting from knowing at least they'd be fighting together. They'd both stand a chance as long as they had each other.

Natalie said, "Okay."

To my surprise, Axel reached out and gently touched a strand of my hair. Time around us stood still as I watched him wrap it around his finger. "I'll get him back to you." He released my hair, watching as it quickly unraveled from around his finger. His eyes drifted to mine. "We'll see you soon."

My lips parted, but I didn't know what to say. Why did it feel like he was actually saying goodbye? Why did it hurt so much? I raised my hand as if to touch him when he pushed me into the passage and quickly closed the door behind us.

I stood there, scared and confused. With the door closed,

I could no longer hear the battle within the house. I could only hear my heavy breathing.

Natalie placed her hand on my shoulder. "We have to go."

I nodded and turned away as we both started running. The only source of light we had was the flashlight in Natalie's hand. I didn't even care about the rats and whatever various insects we ran by...I was too busy trying not to imagine what was happening inside the house.

The ceiling above us shook and dirt and dust fluttered down to us as we paused to brace ourselves in case the ceiling caved in. Natalie looked back at me, her eyes wide. We started running again, faster this time.

We must have been running for at least ten minutes when Natalie's flashlight revealed a door up ahead. We came to a stop, and Natalie held her finger to her lips. She tapped her ear before turning the flashlight off.

I figured she was listening if anything could be heard from the other side, but I couldn't even see my hands in front of my face. I listened as she started shuffling around, and then I heard a latch pull. Natalie groaned as she started pushing on the door. I lent her what little strength I had left, and we managed to shove the door open.

We emerged in the middle of the forest, the darkness around us only made only a little less so from the moon's light above.

Natalie adjusted her backpack and wrapped her arms around the book in her hand.

We both moved quietly through the trees until we were clear to run again.

Despite not being able to shift like a normal werewolf, Natalie still had amazing speed. I knew she was matching my slower pace to stay by my side, so I pushed all my energy and strength into my legs to drive my body forward.

The same noxious odor from before began to tickle my nostrils. Natalie looked over at me as I met her eyes.

Fuck.

She slowed to a jog, and so did I. "Keep running," she said to me as she shoved the book into my arms and pulled two knives from her waist. I stopped jogging as she did. She hissed, "I said to keep running! I may not be able to transform, but I'm still a werewolf. I can buy you some time to get away. Two of them are coming. Go! Now!"

My body started shaking. I couldn't lose her, too. If she stayed and fought these things, there was no doubt they would murder her. "Come on, Natalie! Axel said we should keep running. Don't do this! You can't fight them."

She turned to me, her eyes turning milky white as her claws began to elongate. "I said go!"

Without warning, a vampire rushed out from the woods behind Natalie while she was facing me.

As I screamed her name, a wolf appeared from out of nowhere, jumping into the air and colliding with the vampire. They fell to the ground in a bundle of claws, fangs, growls, and hisses.

I gripped the book in my hand and started backing away.

Natalie stepped in front of me, as yet another vampire appeared, a woman. Her hair was dark and tussled. She smiled as she looked at me and sniffed the air. She rushed towards us and Natalie charged to intercept her. The vamp swiped her claws at Natalie, who didn't dodge quickly enough. The sharp claws ripped into Natalie's upper arm with ease causing massive gashes, and Natalie slapped the vampire across the face with a deep growl. When the vamp rushed at Natalie again, Natalie drove one of her knives into the bloodsucker's throat before digging her nails into the woman's shoulder. Natalie used the rest of her forward momentum to throw the wailing vampire, sending her skidding along the forest floor.

"For fuck's sake, Ruby! Run!" The unknown wolf that had been fighting the other vampire yelped in pain. The vampire zeroed in on me and flashed his fangs. He rushed forward, but the wolf bit down on his shoulder from behind and flipped him over his back. "Run! Now!"

I turned and ran.

7

RUBY

My tongue felt like old sandpaper and my eyes seemed glued shut by dried tears. I felt sure whatever foul stench I was smelling was coming from me.

I rolled onto my back and winced as a rock poked me. Turning back onto my side, I rubbed at my eyes, the sound of singing birds telling me morning had come.

I'd fallen asleep out of pure exhaustion. I tried to stay awake to keep watch, but sleep won the battle. My hand still gripped one of my daggers, and Axel's book was still pressed to my chest. The events of the night before surfaced in my mind. I sighed and closed my eyes as they stung with tears yet again.

I squeezed the book somewhat before sitting up and wiping at my eyes with the small area of my top not covered in dirt. I looked to the side to find my jacket lying beside me. I must've taken it off to cover myself while I slept.

After I finally did what Natalie said and took off, I ran until I felt like my feet were ready to fall off. I slowed some when I could no longer hear Natalie's fight or smell the vampires because I was a wheezing mess.

Still panicked and knowing vampires might follow me, I found a puddle of mud and muck, stopping to lather myself in it before moving on. I figured it might hide my scent. When I eventually came across a small cave so hidden I had almost missed it, I crawled inside and pulled some broken tree limbs and bush over its opening. It was big enough for me to crouch down in and curl my body into a ball.

As uncomfortable as it had been, I figured I would be as good as dead if I kept moving through the forest. If the gunk on me had done its job to hide my scent, the only thing the vampires would have to do was listen and they would hear me stomping through the forest.

I pushed the branches and bush away from the cave's entrance, pushed the book and my backpack out in front of me and crawled out. Thank god, this wasn't a little critter's home. I would have had more problems than just hiding from vampires.

I shielded my eyes against the brightness of the sun and sat on the ground. My stomach was twisted in knots, and I had a headache the size of Asia.

Are they all dead?

The tears burning my eyes that had been fighting to be free—finally escaped. I'd survived the night, and I was both surprised and exceedingly grateful. Had the others survived as well? I closed my eyes for a moment but opened them quickly as unwelcome images from the night before began to flash before my eyes.

I swallowed whatever drops of saliva had been produced in my mouth, my only source of water I had since I had finished my bottle of water last night. I pulled myself up off the ground and groaned because my body ached all over. I had to get back to the pack. I needed to know if the others were okay. I started to walk slowly through the forest.

After I had been walking for a while, I stopped when I spotted a tiny pool of water that had settled in one of the curved leaves of a plant. I dipped my pinkie finger in first and tapped it on my tongue. I shrugged. It tasted like plain old water. I drank it, hoping it was just water from the light rain of last night.

I rocked back on my heels somewhat. It felt like I hadn't tasted water in decades. I was about to keep walking straight when my eyes caught sight of something brownish red splashed on some bushes to my left. I frowned and went in that direction. As I followed the little colored trail, I realized what I was looking at: blood.

My heart started pounding as I came upon a spot drenched in ruddy brown. The metallic smell of blood had me pressing my tongue to the roof of my mouth to stop myself from gagging. I looked around me and my knees grew weak. This was where I had left Natalie, I was certain of it.

I turned in a circle, growing lightheaded at the sight of the blood-soaked ground. I didn't want to wonder if this was all her blood. I took off running, pushing myself despite my pain and exhaustion. Soon I spotted the house through the trees.

"Finally," I panted, and I continued running towards the front of the house.

I eyed the broken front door, hanging at an odd angle. I set Axel's book and my bag down to prepare myself to enter. I had no idea what I might find. Just in case a vampire was lingering around, I pulled out both my daggers. I quickly slammed the damaged front door and held my daggers out in a fighting stance, ready to defend myself against any remaining bloodsuckers. But I heard nothing, and nothing moved. The house was in shambles with blood on the floor and walls. Even with my normal human hearing, if a pin had dropped, I would have been able to hear it in the echoing silence.

After I was satisfied that no monsters were there to jump out and attack me, I relaxed my stance and checked out my surroundings. I walked down the hall we had run down last night, but I didn't get far. The walls and floors were saturated in blood. I closed my eyes and stepped back. *I need to find them! I have to find them!*

What if the vampires took them?

I returned to the lobby and turned in the direction of the kitchen when I came face to face with Mathieu.

He looked me up and down.

"Where are they?" I asked instantly. I knew I looked like a wreck and smelled like the sewer, but I'd never been so happy to see someone. "Where are they, Mathieu? Please tell me they're okay." I stepped forward, my hands now shaking. Somehow, seeing him made me even more emotional. Maybe it was the regretful look in his eyes. I didn't want to start thinking the worst, but if he didn't start talking soon, I would lose my shit.

His dark eyes, so much like Xavier's, drifted away from me.

"Mathieu?" I asked.

"Come with me."

He'd been a man of few words since the moment I had

met him, but his silence right now was too much to bear. If Xavier were badly hurt or dead, wouldn't he be losing his mind right now? He'd lost his wife and barely survived that. I didn't want to think about what would happen to Mathieu if he lost Xavier too.

I exhaled a breath I hadn't known I was holding. Xavier must be okay.

I hoped.

"Can you just tell me what happened, please?"

"Xavier was badly wounded. So was Axel, but they are both healing quickly," He explained as we arrived on the second floor. He turned to face me.

I waited for him to say something about Natalie, but he added nothing else. "And Natalie?" I asked as I bent my head back to look up at him.

He combed his midnight hair back and turned away. He looked exhausted and his thick beard seemed to now have more grey hairs than black. "I'll take you to her."

I didn't like the sound of that. We walked in silence until we got to her bedroom. He held onto the door handle before looking back at me. "Don't try to wake her, okay?"

I frowned but nodded.

"You can go in." He opened the door.

I stepped around him to enter. When I saw her, my hand flew to my mouth. A very pale Natalie was lying completely still on her back in the bed dressed in a clean white nightgown. As I stepped further into the room, I could see multiple teeth marks on her ankle, wrist, and arms.

I had to look closely to see that her chest was rising and falling slowly. She looked dead. I started crying. I couldn't stop the tears this time as they flowed down my cheeks.

Mathieu entered the room and placed his hand on my shoulder.

I hunched forward as I covered my mouth to silence my sobs. "Is s-she—dying?" I whispered to him.

"No," he replied. Although he whispered, his voice was still loud enough to hear clearly. "But she's in a coma. They almost killed her."

I held both my daggers in my left hand as I used the back of my right hand to wipe at my tears. My hand fell to my side as I stepped away from him. I placed my daggers on the ground unceremoniously and carried a chair next to Natalie's bed. I sat down heavily, my eyes roaming over her motionless body as my fists clenched in anger.

Mathieu left, closing the door soundlessly behind him.

I reached out and held her hand gently, my eyes tearing up once more at the bite marks at her wrist. The wounds were closed and almost healed, but the bruised skin around the punctures still appeared bright, especially with how white she looked.

"Natalie, it's Ruby. I hope you can hear me. I'm right here with you," I reassured her. I wasn't sure if she could hear me while in a coma, but I figured it couldn't hurt for her to know she wasn't alone.

Her long hair looked as white as the pillow beneath her head. Despite the evidence of injuries, she looked utterly angelic. She was the first true friend I'd ever had. After my traumatic introduction into the supernatural world, Natalie had been someone I knew I could trust, no matter what.

I should have forced her to run with me or stayed to fight with her. I shook my head in helpless resignation as fresh tears fell from my eyes. No, I couldn't have fought with her. I would have been more of a liability than an asset. Nevertheless, I felt sick of always being the one who had to run and leave everyone else behind to fight and die!

I wiped at my tears. "I'm right here. I'm okay, and you will be, too." I rubbed my thumb against her hand. "Wake up soon, please."

Ruby

I woke up with horrible pain in my neck. I had fallen asleep sitting down beside Natalie with my head resting on the edge of the bed.

I stared at her for a moment before getting up and stretching. My clothes felt stiff and I didn't even want to think about how horrible I smelled. Mathieu had said Xavier and Axel were okay, and I doubted they would mind if I took a shower before looking for them.

It must have taken an hour for me to scrub my body and hair fully clean. The floor of the shower was black by the time I finished. Once I finally made it out of the shower, I felt refreshed. I dried my hair with a towel and braided my hair into a single plait down my back before searching the house for Xavier.

He wasn't on the second floor. As I carefully made my way around ripped paintings and shattered décor in the ravaged halls of the third floor, I soon heard talking. I sped up and stopped at a door left slightly ajar, revealing Mathieu and Xavier inside. I watched as they skimmed through the pages of the book I had carried back with me.

Xavier was shirtless with a large bandage wrapped around his abdomen along with other bandages on his left arm and right shoulder. I smiled as I observed him, and my smile widened when he looked up and saw me.

His long legs carried him to me within seconds as I entered the room. He pulled me into a tight hug that lifted me completely off the ground. If he had squeezed any tighter, he would have crushed me, but I didn't care as I squeezed him back with all my strength. I felt like crying again but managed to hold it in. I'd done more than my share of crying lately, enough to last a lifetime. I hated how I was becoming a crybaby, but this shit was getting to me.

Maybe it was because I never had people I cared about this much. I never had to fear losing anyone. I never had to stress and wonder if someone I cared about was okay.

"I came to look for you but you were sleeping," he said to me as he placed me back onto the floor. "You looked like shit."

I laughed and shrugged. "I figured if I covered myself in mud, all the vampires wouldn't smell me."

He nodded. "I guess that makes sense. One might have come after you except they were all taken care of." He looked down at his abdomen. "It wasn't easy."

I ran a finger gently over the bandage on his shoulder, arm, and then his face. He didn't look like he was in pain as he looked down at me with a smile on his lips, but I couldn't help feeling bad seeing him injured like this.

"I'm all right." He leaned forward and kissed my forehead. "I'm glad you're safe. Natalie said you had gotten away before she fell unconscious. I was out cold after her." He walked back over to Mathieu. "Axel patched us up as much as he could until Dad got here."

I followed him. "What are you guys doing?" I asked as I gazed down at the book. "Did you find anything useful?"

Xavier placed his hand on the table as he leaned over the book next to me. Its pages were a yellow shade with gold designs around its edges. "Axel was right. Stakes don't work on vampires. Beheading and burning them works, so yes to sunlight and UV lights."

"Vampires were around in my great, great, great, great, great grandfather's time," Mathieu said as he turned one of the pages. Both left and right pages together made up a large picture of a battle between vampires and werewolves. "I never believed the stories about vampires. Some supernaturals have traits like a vampire. I always assumed someone simply mistook one of those other supernaturals for a vampire." He ran his hand gently over the page. "I didn't know Axel's family had this book." He sighed. "Either way, it makes sense vampires would become stories if they've been gone…well, in hiding for all these years."

"The Council must have records on them. They could have told us all the stories were true," Xavier pointed out as he crossed his arms in front of his chest.

Mathieu nodded. "Yes, but they wouldn't have felt the need to come out and say yes, vampires were once real. They were thought to be extinct. The Council doesn't care if wolves believe they existed or not. It's not like having the flu and taking shots to prevent it from happening again. The species was thought to be wiped out, gone…no longer a threat."

Xavier exhaled heavily through his nose and turned away.

I understood what Xavier was trying to say, but Mathieu was also right. Why protect oneself against something you thought could never happen? The thought wouldn't even cross your mind.

"It sucks that countless packs are defenseless now," Xavier muttered. "They're going to be picked off one by one. How can we get this info to everyone in time?"

"Make a video," I offered. The words were out my mouth before I even thought about what I was really saying. I cleared my throat as Xavier turned around. "I mean, if the Council won't release any information, you have to share what you know. You've fought them and survived. Explain everything you know in the video and show them the book as well."

His eyes turned to slits as he held his chin and appeared to seriously consider my words. He looked over at his father.

Mathieu stared back at him and nodded.

"That's not a bad idea," Xavier said. "Sometimes, the simplest approach is best. I'll have it sent to all the alphas I know and they can then help with distributing it."

"I suggest doing it while you still have those bandages on," I added.

Xavier frowned. "No. I am the Alpha-to-be for the Black-moon Pack. I can't show weakness, not even now."

I shook my head. "It's not a weakness. It'll help bring across the message that these creatures should not be underestimated. And since you've already fought them and only came away with these wounds, you shouldn't be underestimated either. You're not an Alpha yet, but you are strong. Once this is all over and you do become the alpha, everyone will look up to you. You would have given everyone the vital information they needed to survive when the Council didn't."

"She's right," Mathieu recognized as he placed his hand on Xavier's shoulder. "It's about time the leadership transfer was done anyways, but with everything happening, it'll have to wait. I've served as Alpha long enough and have made my mark. It's time you secure your future. You know many packs don't like us because we still protect humans. Respect will be earned once we step forward and help them to survive this."

"Okay, I'll do it," Xavier agreed as he closed the book. He sent a proud smile my way. "I'll make the video now before we leave."

I smiled as my cheeks heated up. *Maybe I wouldn't make such a bad Luna after all.* "Where is Axel?" I asked. I wanted to see him as well. According to what Xavier had said, Axel was the one who took care of both him and Natalie in the end.

Xavier frowned somewhat but said nothing as Mathieu replied, "He's helping Randoll with burying the bodies of the wolves that were killed last night. The vampire bodies are being burned."

"Did any wolves survive?" I asked.

Mathieu nodded. "Two others survived. They are helping Randoll and Axel." His face twisted with anger. "Those things destroyed my home. This house has been in the Blackwood family for years, and now all I smell is vampire filth."

"None of them escaped," Xavier told him.

I jumped for joy on the inside. I wished I could learn to fight so I could be of some help, but there was no time to spare to train me to take on a vampire. Most of the wolves outside of Axel's pack were only just learning how to combat vampires themselves.

"How did you kill them?" I questioned Xavier. What if I was ever attacked again and there was no one around to help me? I really needed to be ready, just in case. I understood vampires' weaknesses, so at least that was a start for me.

"In wolf form, I aimed for the head. Ripped it clean off. Once they've been fully decapitated, they are done for."

I nodded. "I need a gun."

Xavier raised a brow as the side of his mouth curved into a look of amusement.

I knew what that look meant. I was just a girl, so why would anyone trust me with a gun? "Yes, I do know how to use a gun, Xavier, so don't be so sexist. I had to stay with a lot of different types of families growing up thanks to the foster care system. Most of the time it wasn't pretty, but some of the foster parents were nicer than others. In one of the better homes, I had a foster Dad named Dave that worked for the FBI. He took me to the gun range and taught me how to shoot. I wasn't half bad at it either."

The smile on his face transformed into a look of surprise.

"I may not be able to bite a vampire's head off, but I sure as hell can shoot one."

His mouth turned upside down as he made a face. "Hmm, all right then, fair enough."

Dave's home had been just about the only one I had stayed in that I didn't hate. I had only stayed with them for a few months, but it hadn't been too bad. Unfortunately, right when I was just starting to have a little hope that maybe I could really stay with them for a while and be happy, the foster mom—Alicia—got cancer. They couldn't take care of me anymore, so it was on to the next placement for me. Other than the men that stood here with me, Natalie and yes, Axel as well, Dave and Alicia were the only ones I'd ever given a shit about in my life. It was strange—I'd only know the wolves for a relatively short time, yet they were already like the family I'd never had. "Is Natalie going to be okay?" I asked suddenly.

Xavier's eyes darkened. "I don't know," he replied as he pressed his fingers into his eyes. "Axel had gotten to her just in time before she could be drained."

None of us spoke and for me, I couldn't because I was too pissed to speak. Natalie didn't deserve this. No one deserved anything like this. A growl made me jump, and I realized it was Mathieu.

His eyes turned black and he looked away.

I stared at him. She was his niece, almost like a daughter to him, and he'd already lost so much. My heart went out to him, but I dared not say anything to comfort him. I feared he might interpret it as pity. It didn't seem like Alphas were big on displaying emotions, not ones that made them appear vulnerable anyways.

He looked down at his watch. "It's 8 am. It'll take a few hours for us to drive to the location where the others are, so I suggest we leave within the next hour."

"Can Natalie travel in her current state?" I asked him.

He sighed and walked away. "She has to," he answered and left the room.

I turned to Xavier and he called me to him softly. My body moved to him instantly as if he had stuck a hook inside me and was reeling me in. He wrapped his arms around me and I sagged against him. His body felt like a warm heating pad. I closed my eyes, relaxing into his touch.

He kissed the top of my head. "Do you want to help me with making the video? We have to do it quickly."

I nodded. "Sure," I replied in a low voice.

He leaned away slightly and brought a long finger up under my chin, gently moving it upward until my eyes met his. "I'm glad you're okay, Ruby. I don't know what I'd have done if those things had gotten to you."

"Oh, it would only be a matter of time before you got another girlfriend." I chuckled.

His face fell.

Mine did too, as I stared back at him.

Suddenly, a wide grin appeared on his lips.

"What?"

"So, you're my girlfriend?"

My eyes widened. *Did I just say that?* I tried to step away from him, but he tightened his hands around me. His lips swiftly claimed mine, and I immediately stopped trying to move away from him. All of sudden, it felt as if I could never get close enough. I moaned softly into his mouth as his large hands found their way under my shirt at my waistline. I reveled in the feel of his soft warmth as he smoothly caressed the sensitive skin of the curves of my abdomen.

He pulled away unexpectedly, and I screamed on the inside for more. When I gazed up at him, his eyes were black and his fangs had appeared. My heartbeat sped up even faster.

"Don't be frightened. My wolf just wanted to taste you too." He lightly kissed my cheek and then my shoulder.

I shivered as his tongue swiped against my skin.

"We should make the video before I lose focus entirely."

I swallowed and nodded.

He pinched my chin suddenly. "And never joke about me replacing you, or you dying for that matter. Understood?"

I nodded yet again, my tongue too heavy to answer all of a sudden.

Xavier smiled. "Good girl."

8

RUBY

*A*fter I finished helping Xavier with the video, I went back to Natalie's room to check on her. Her backpack from the night before was sitting by the door, covered in blood. I unpacked her things and placed them all in a new clean bag.

I got her dressed before returning to my room to collect my bag. I took Natalie's and my bags down to the car before I headed back inside. All the while, I was lost in thought.

Watching Xavier make that video had been a proud moment for me. He had looked so strong, so confident. He wore his scars like a warrior. I knew everyone who saw the video would heed his warnings and be thankful for his pointers on how to survive.

It wasn't a big deal in the grand scheme of things, but it was rewarding to know that I had given him the idea to do the video. I had contributed something essential to the survival of other werewolves. I was more than just the helpless human mate, needing protection, and serving no purpose. Fuck that! I was useful, and I had proved it.

I sighed as I plopped down on my bed, a blush making its way up my neck to my cheeks. I had called myself his girlfriend. Even though the moment had already passed, I covered my face in embarrassment just thinking about it. I couldn't believe I'd made that slip.

He seemed more than pleased about it, though. And that kiss...oh man, that kiss...I could still taste him on my lips.

I was his mate, but we had never talked about me being his Luna or even his girlfriend, for that matter. I smiled. Well, it looked like I was officially off the market. I chuckled to myself as I inhaled deeply and then exhaled. I got up and turned in a circle. I had a feeling I wouldn't be coming back to this house for a while or maybe ever.

When this all ended, the house would need a lot of renovation to return to its former glory. The stench of blood inside the house would fade over time, but the walls and floor would be permanently stained with blood. There was no time to clean it all up before we left. No wonder Mathieu was so pissed—the house had been his family for generations. I frowned. I shouldn't have given a damn about this house right now. The house would be fine. I needed to focus on getting out of here and safely indoors again before nightfall.

"See you," I said to my room as I walked out and closed the door. I went to Natalie's room, but she was no longer there. I figured Xavier must have taken her down to the car, so they must have been waiting on me.

As I headed to the first floor, I stepped around a corner and came face to face with Axel.

His hair hung loosely around his shoulders, damp with sweat. He was also shirtless, red scars covering his body, probably from the battle the night before. A bandage wrapped around his side as well, but for the most part, he looked fine. His chest glistening with sweat rose as he inhaled. "How are you?"

I shrugged. "Not great, but I'm alive." I pointed at his side. " How are you?"

He peered down at his side. "Yeah, I'm good. I've been worse. That bite was just a little deeper than the others. I heard what you did to stay safe out there last night. I wish I could have seen you, covered in mud and all."

I rolled my eyes. "Of course, you would."

He chuckled. "That was smart thinking."

I looked away, not wanting him to see that I was blushing. A compliment or praise from Axel was rare. "Uh, thanks," I replied simply. Neither of us spoke after that as I looked back at him. I soon looked away again, unable to handle the awkwardness and his piercing stare. Seeing him well had caused me to feel happier, though. "So…" I drawled. "Your pack is safe, right?"

He moved his hair behind his ears. "Yeah, they're all safe. My pack isn't as large as the Blackmoon Pack, so it wasn't hard to move them all. They're at another safe house like the one we were at. A warlock's warding protects them."

I crossed my arms over my chest as I narrowed my eyes at him. "You seem to have a lot of warlocks on your payroll. What's up with that?"

He smirked down at me. "You don't need to worry your pretty little red head about that, Ruby." He crossed his arms over his broad chest and leaned on the wall. "I will be checking on that witch to see if she can help you, though. I keep my promises."

84

I held his stare this time. "So, I guess you're not coming with us then?" Since he wasn't dressed, it was clear he wasn't prepared to go anywhere, but I still asked.

He'd done a lot for Xavier and me as it was. Despite the feud between them and the tension between all three of us, his recent actions spoke volumes about his character. Xavier had said Axel had saved both him and Natalie in the end. I wouldn't tell him this, but having him travel with us would have made me feel just a little safer. "You have to stay with them to keep them safe, even behind a warlock's warding," I added quickly, so I didn't sound like a child about to cry when their mother leaves for work.

He narrowed his eyes at me and stepped forward rapidly, leaving but a small gap between us.

I held my breath.

"Why? Will you miss me, Ruby?"

I blinked, then blinked again while still holding my breath. Why did Axel sound like that just now? I frowned. Why was he looking at me like this? Why was I being affected? Butterflies began to flap their wings furiously inside me, and I stood up straight to hold my composure. "No," I answered and managed to keep a straight face.

His eyes roamed over my face, but he made no move to step away from me. He leaned in further, his nose almost touching mine. "I can tell when you're lying. Your voice becomes too low." He tilted his head to the side.

I stared into the depths of his hazel eyes.

He didn't look away, but I did as he raised a hand to hold a strand of hair by my face. I looked back at him as his jaws clenched, and he slowly released the strand. "Don't worry, I'll miss you too."

I wanted to snort or laugh or say something witty, but I couldn't. He was too close to me. I feared if I spoke, my lips might accidentally touch his. What a disaster that would be! My eyes flicked down to his lips as he licked them, and my heart skipped a beat.

His gaze stayed locked on my face. "I meant what I said earlier. You did well with hiding yourself. You should keep those daggers on you at all times. Xavier will protect you with his life, I know," he said that with a little venom in his voice. "But like last night, you might have to fend for yourself at some point. You have to be able to protect yourself. Do you understand?"

What was with these men and asking me if I understand? I wasn't incompetent. I reached behind me and removed the dagger I'd shoved into my waistband. I brandished it and pressed the tip under his chin. "Don't worry about me, Axel. I'll be just fine. I'm stronger than I look."

The corner of his mouth curved until it turned into a full-blown smile.

I was surprised to see a dimple appear on his left cheek. For someone always so serious, seeing him smile was like seeing the sun after months of rain. I would tell him to smile more, except I didn't want it to go to his head.

He moved to the side to whisper in my ear, "I know. A weak woman would never be my mate."

My heart stopped as he moved to stare at me once more. His eyes drifted down to my lips, and a ringing started in my ear as I began to panic. Was he going to kiss me? What would I do if he did? Was it cheating if he was my mate as well?

Someone cleared their throat, and I stepped away from Axel as if he had burned me.

Axel sighed and looked behind him to find Xavier standing a few steps away from us.

I couldn't tell what the look in Xavier's eyes meant—if he was angry or not. He merely looked at Axel and then back at me.

"Are you ready? We need to get going," Axel said.

I nodded, unable to speak from embarrassment. What had I just almost allowed to happen?

Axel looked back at me.

I gave him a tight-lipped smile. "Be safe."

"I will," he replied. "I'll come and find you after I've checked on my people, and I have information from that witch."

I nodded and stepped around him to join Xavier.

Xavier nodded at Axel.

Axel slowly returned the nod.

We moved away. Though I wanted to look back behind me, I didn't. I could feel Axel's eyes on me, though.

Xavier and I headed down to the car in silence. I felt uncomfortable. What was he thinking about? How much of Axel's and my conversation had he heard?

I shook my head mentally as we walked through the front door. It wasn't like we had been talking about anything secret. I needed to get my shit together and stop being awkward. Being awkward might cause Xavier to think more had transpired than what actually had.

Natalie's head was resting in the seat of the car I was to sit in.

Xavier opened the car door for me and then gently held Natalie's head up for me so I could sit down. I then placed a small pillow on my lap to rest her head on. I felt uncomfortable having her traveling like this, but I knew there was no other choice.

Xavier closed the door softly and got into the front.

Mathieu maneuvered the car away from the house.

Randoll had left long ago with the two wolves that had survived, so it was just us three.

As we drove down the long driveway to get to the main road, I moved Natalie's hair out of her face and placed my hand on her cheek to keep her head from moving around. An IV drip with fluids was attached to her arm and anchored to the seat that I was keeping an eye on as well.

"Is there anyone in the pack that might be able to help her?" I asked Mathieu.

He shook his head. "Right now, all we can do is keep her comfortable."

A sound echoed in the car, and I assumed Xavier had hit something with his hand. "Reika, we should have called her! She should know how to help Natalie."

"I hadn't thought about her either," Mathieu said as he dug into his pants pocket and pulled out his phone. "Call her, see what she knows." He glanced behind him at Natalie and me before looking back at the road. He turned left as we got to the highway. "Maybe she can mind-link Natalie. See how she's doing mentally."

I cracked my window a little then drifted off into my own world as he drove. My head lulled back against the seat, and I closed my eyes. Even though I had slept last night, I still felt drained.

I just prayed Reika could help. I couldn't do any of this without Natalie. Not only that, but I also knew she did so much for this pack. Losing her would most definitely send everyone into despair. Considering how powerful she had become of late, I wouldn't be surprised if things would get much darker for the pack in this conflict with the vampires if we lost her.

I didn't know exactly how things worked with their goddess, like if wolves prayed to her the same way humans pray to their god. Nevertheless, I sent a prayer to their goddess to protect Natalie anyway. I just hoped she accepted prayers from humans too.

Xavier

I rested my elbow heavily on the window as Dad stepped on the gas. I could tell he was starting to become uneasy because it was already almost 4 pm. I checked on Ruby in the mirror on the door, only to see her gazing out her window.

I had heard what Axel had said to her—only a strong woman could be his mate. I didn't disagree with him because I believed the same for myself. I still wanted to rip his spine out, though. He'd stood far too close to her when he'd whispered it. For so long, Axel had denied his feelings for her, but I could hear them loud and clear in his voice back there.

He wanted her, and there was no hiding it anymore.

I closed my eyes as the breeze tickled my face. Over time, I'd slowly become less pissed whenever I saw them talking. At first, the mere mention of the fact that I was not Ruby's only mate would enrage me. Since I couldn't allow this thing between the three of us to drive me insane, all I could do was accept the way things were. It still pained me to see her with him, but at the end of the day, she was more mine than his—for now anyways.

However, I was no fool. I knew what the wolf bond was like, and I knew she must have had some lingering feelings for him. I trusted that our bond was stronger than the two of theirs. I wasn't sure what I would do if I ever saw Axel kiss Ruby. It would cut me to my core, but I knew I wouldn't be able to kick his ass or be angry with her.

The bond pulls mates together, and that couldn't be helped. I could only imagine how he felt seeing her with me.

The moment I was about to dial Reika's number, she called on Dad's phone. She instantly asked for Natalie and said she had gotten a bad feeling about her. I shouldn't have been surprised. Reika was a powerful Enchanted, much like Natalie. I filled her in on what had happened. As soon as I told her vampires had attacked the house, she asked me if Ruby was safe. I paused for a moment, finding it strange that she seemed so concerned for Ruby, specifically.

Catching my sudden hesitation, Reika clarified that keeping Ruby safe was extremely important, despite what was going on around us. She was the first human to be mated to a wolf. She and I—and Axel—were making history.

Reika advised us not to force Natalie out of her coma. It could be done, but it wasn't something she recommended. If she dove into Natalie's psyche now, it would be dangerous for them both. Unfortunately, Natalie would have to wake up on her own terms. Reika offered to hop on a plane to aid us since Natalie was out of commission. I refused her offer.

Natalie trusted her, but I didn't. I knew Reika still worked for Olcan. She was too close to the Council for my comfort. Natalie had told me all about how she had played a part in helping Ruby and me to escape, but I refused to trust her completely. Reika recognized that I was wary, yet she didn't seem to hold it against us.

"Thank you, Reika, but I think you remaining there would be wise. We'll be able to keep track of what the Council is doing. If you leave to come to our aid, the Council will turn their attention to you, assuming that you've betrayed them."

Reika saw the wisdom of my words and told me she would keep me updated. For now, all she knew was that Olcan didn't seem too shaken up about vampires still being alive. She told me to keep her updated on Natalie, and our call ended.

I hadn't said this to her, but I wouldn't be surprised if Olcan had known all along about vampires still being alive. The rumor was that the vampires hadn't tried to kill him and instead only attacked other Council members.

"Reika helped Natalie the night you left. She placed Olcan and me under a sleeping spell," Dad guessed after my call with Reika ended.

"If you weren't asleep, would you have stopped Ruby and me from leaving?" I asked him.

He didn't answer right away.

I turned to look at him.

"No," he finally answered. "I wouldn't have stopped the two of you. I didn't need to hear it from Olcan to know he wanted Ruby dead."

"Then why were you so relaxed about the whole thing?

You were willing to let us go with him knowing what the outcome would be."

He looked over at me, a deep crease between his brows. "You think I would let Olcan hurt my only son? Acting outright against Olcan would be foolish, but I had no intention of letting him kill you or Ruby."

I felt bad for asking him a question like that. The thump of an erratic heartbeat pulled me from my thoughts, and I frowned. A pained moaning sound met my ears from the backseat, and I hastily glanced behind me to see Natalie trying to move her hand.

Ruby looked at me with wide eyes before placing her hand lightly on Natalie's chest. "Natalie?" she whispered to her. "Natalie? Can you hear me?"

Natalie's head moved from side to side as her heartbeat increased rapidly.

"Dad, slow down!" I called to him.

He slowed the car down to a snail's pace.

Ruby caressed Natalie's hair. "Natalie?"

Her heartbeat started to slow down again, and she stopped moving soon after. I released a breath I hadn't realized I had been holding.

"What was that?" Ruby asked.

I shrugged. "I don't know. Maybe she's slowly waking up," I answered before facing forward again. "Maybe I should have told Reika to come after all."

Dad sped up a little as he checked his watch. "We're running out of time."

"I know that, but…" I froze, my ears twitching as Natalie started to mumble. I turned my head around swiftly to look at her again.

Sweat formed on her forehead as she continued to mumble under her breath.

"Xavier?" Ruby called—her face twisted with worry. "What's wrong with her?" She placed her hand on Natalie's cheek. "Natalie, can you hear me? It's Ruby." She reached down to hold Natalie's hand. "Squeeze my hand if you can hear me."

Nothing happened, but Natalie continued to mumble. Soon she started to shake. Under her lids, I could see her eyes darting from left to right frantically.

Ruby released her hand as Natalie started to twist and turn. "She's going to rip the needle out of her arm if she keeps doing this!" Ruby cautioned hurriedly.

I leaned over just as Natalie's eyes popped open. I paused as I felt a burst of relief to see her awake. Sadly, that relief was short-lived. Before I had time to say anything to her, she started screaming. The scream was so high pitched, I felt my blood immediately rush to my ears. I covered them hastily and fell back into my seat.

Ruby covered her ears. Thanks to the fact that she didn't have the heightened senses of a werewolf, Ruby didn't seem to be as affected as my father and I were.

The car started to sway as blood poured from my dad's ears. My vision started to blur as the scream continued to flow from her lips like something from a horror movie. I could feel a burst of power in the car, and my dad hunched forward with a pained growl as blood dripped from the side of my mouth.

I felt like I was being crushed from the inside out. *What kind of power is this?* I swung around to her again. "Natalie! Stop! Natalie!"

Natalie stopped screaming abruptly. Her hand flew to Ruby's face to hold her forehead. Blood instantly began to roll down Ruby's face where Natalie's nails were digging into her.

Ruby's eyes widened, and so did mine. I grabbed at Natalie to release her hold on Ruby. "Natalie, what the fuck are you doing? You're hurting her."

Ruby's mouth fell open, and her eyes turned white as she started to scream.

Natalie groaned as her head swayed from side to side, and she started screaming once again.

I held my head. It felt like my brain was about to explode. I turned back around to face forward. As dad lost control of the swaying car, I was thrown forward, my head slamming against the dashboard.

"The-they're—going to—kill us," my dad said as he coughed, and blood splashed onto the steering wheel.

This couldn't be happening! What the fuck was happening?!

I reached around my seat and grabbed onto Natalie. I didn't want to do this, but I had no choice. I held her throat and pressed down—she instantly fell unconscious. I just hoped I didn't send her back into a coma.

Was she even really awake, or was she doing this in her sleep?

Natalie's hand fell away from Ruby's face, and her head lulled to the side as her eyes rolled back.

The car skidded to a halt in the middle of the road, and I pressed my fingers into my temples. My heart felt like it was trying to beat its way right out of my chest.

Dad panted loudly beside me as he touched his ear and nose, his finger coming away with blood. He shook his head a little, no doubt feeling disoriented like me. He glanced behind him at Ruby and Natalie before looking at me.

We could both hear them breathing just fine, but when I looked at Ruby, blood started to run from her nose.

Dad started the car again and pulled over to the side of the road.

Ruby's eyes opened, showing her normal green eyes before they changed back to white once more. She started to mutter, her eyes twitching. She began feeling around the car door and pulled the door open, forcing Dad to stop the vehicle suddenly as she stumbled out.

I jumped out as well and rushed to her, scooping her up in my arms. "Ruby?" I moved her hair back from her face and patted her cheek gently as her eyes started to close. "Stay with me. Stay with me, baby."

Dad hopped out of the car to check on Natalie.

I was close to losing my shit as Ruby kept muttering incoherent words, and blood started running from her eyes as they closed. "Fuck! Dad! What's wrong with her?"

He rushed over to me.

Gasping for air abruptly, Ruby bolted upright and out of my arms. She was wheezing with her heavy breathing as she started looking around frantically.

"Ruby! Ruby, calm down, I'm here!"

Her eyes looked as if she widened them any further, they would pop from her face. She began wiping her face, seeming confused as to why she was covered in blood. Her eyes teared up.

I felt like howling because I didn't know what to do to help her. *What had Natalie done to her?*

My dad's piercing howl suddenly rang out around us.

Ruby jumped, her eyes streaming with tears, but she stopped panicking and looked at me. "The-they're all—going t-to die," she stammered, her eyes still as white as the clouds above us.

What the hell is she talking about?

"Who? Who is going to die?" Dad asked as he stooped down.

Whimpering, Ruby closed her eyes and held her head as she moaned. More tears flooded her eyes. "They're all going to die."

9

RUBY

*J*t took a while for me to start breathing normally again. I desperately wanted to calm down, I just couldn't.

Xavier sat with me while all the adrenaline inside me took it's time to return to normal.

Then I was speechless. It's not that I didn't want to talk, but…I just couldn't form the words necessary to answer any of Xavier's or Mathieu's questions. I was still in shock.

After twenty minutes, Mathieu told us we needed to get back on the road because it would be nightfall soon, and we had a good bit of traveling left. So, we all piled back into the car. We drove with a horrible silence hanging over our heads.

Natalie was still out cold. Mathieu and Xavier were busy cleaning the blood off themselves with wet wipes.

I just sat in the back, staring out the window. I knew Xavier kept glancing at me through his mirror since it was positioned to see the back window. I pretended not to see him, though. I wasn't ready to talk yet.

I peered down at Natalie on my lap as she slept soundly

before looking away once more. Pinching the bridge of my nose, I groaned. My stomach felt weird, and I felt a tingling vibration under my skin.

"Ruby?"

I glanced up to see Xavier staring at me.

His neck twisted oddly since he was looking at me through the small space between his seat and the door. "You okay?"

My lips curved with a weak smile as I nodded, and I could see the relief in his eyes. I started to feel bad.

He had no idea what just happened. He turned around in his seat as much as he could to poke his head around to the backseat. "What happened?"

I sighed as I gazed down at Natalie, noticing a little more color appearing on her pale skin.

"I'm not sure, but I had a vision," I replied in a low voice. "She held me. Then this world, the car, and everything else washed away and was replaced."

"Replaced by what?" Mathieu probed.

I looked up and blinked several times. "A town or city, I don't know, but it was night time. There was smoke, a lot of smoke." I swallowed. "There were vampires killing people."

Xavier's brows instantly knitted at the mention of vampires.

I went on to describe it, "They were ripped to pieces…all those people. There was blood everywhere."

Xavier looked at his father as Mathieu returned the glance.

"I could a-almost feel their pain and fear—i-it was horrible," I added.

Xavier stared at me with such pity.

I shook my head and sat up straight. Seeing those people killed like that, like animals being slaughtered, had made me feel sick to my stomach. Maybe this was why I couldn't get rid of this odd feeling, this tingling all over my body. I decided not to mention the feeling. I was really okay, and Xavier and Mathieu didn't need anything else to worry about.

Xavier looked like he was ready to lock me in a room for the rest of my life. "I'm sorry," he said.

I smiled at him. I hoped it showed him I was fine. "It's okay. I don't know if it was something that already happened or is going to happen, but it felt like I was there."

Mathieu unexpectedly sped the car up, and I quickly placed my hand on Natalie's shoulder to keep her steady.

"It's almost dark," he told us. "We need to get off the road as soon as possible. We have only an hour left to get to the location, and it's almost dark. With Natalie unconscious, if we're attacked, they'll go for her first."

"Okay," Xavier replied. "Not too fast though. We really can't have her doing what she just did a second time. None of us will survive it."

"What happened to you two anyway?" I asked. "You started bleeding from just her screaming. I mean, it was loud, but—"

"It was louder for us," Xavier interjected. "Humans can't hear dog whistles, but it drives dogs nuts and wolves too. That's what it was like. There was a high-pitched ringing in my ear." He looked down at Natalie. "She's never done that before."

"She's getting stronger," Mathieu stated. "She gained a lot of power in a short space of time. It's not like she's been nurturing these gifts to this level gradually. It'll take some time for her to get the hang of it. What happened just now was quite strange, I admit."

Xavier faced forward again and placed his elbow on the window. "That was a lot of power. I've never heard of an Enchanted doing anything like what she just did. No one knows what she's capable of, but Enchanteds usually don't have offensive powers." He snorted. "Well, that was one hell of a mental attack. It felt like my brain was going to be liquefied."

Mathieu removed one hand from the steering wheel to press his fingers into the corner of his eyes. It seemed apparent he was still feeling some lingering effects of Natalie's attack. "If she saw what Ruby just explained, and Ruby reacted the way she did, it makes sense Natalie panicked like that." He placed his hand back onto the steering wheel, and the car accelerated a little more. "I've seen her have visions only to wake up and find cuts on her body as if she actually experienced what she'd seen. Sometimes while in a vision, what she sees will be real enough for her to feel the need to protect herself. Although Enchanteds never experience the pain of shifting, they still go through more than their fair share of suffering."

I again gazed down at Natalie. It seemed too hard to be an Enchanted. I couldn't imagine being plagued with visions of horrible things while knowing there was nothing I could do about them. Right now, I felt sick to my stomach and uncomfortable. If that vision showed the future, all those people were going to be slaughtered.

I wanted to stop it. I wanted to help them. How had Natalie ever managed to live with seeing something so depressing yet still managed to keep even a part of her cheerful demeanor?

I missed the old Natalie. I missed that joyful, perky girl I had met not so long ago. She'd been so quiet and distant in comparison ever since the transfer. I guess with everything happening, it was enough to change anyone. I felt like I was watching her being stripped of her happiness.

"She lashed out because it was too real," Xavier affirmed. "But she shared her vision with Ruby. I know an Enchanted can show someone the memory of a vision, but I thought they couldn't share their visions while they were happening. Apparently, we have much to learn about Enchanteds who have received power transfers."

"I could feel them dying, that's why I lashed out," Natalie suddenly spoke.

I jumped as I looked down and saw her blue eyes staring up at me.

Xavier swung around in his seat to stare down at her.

I glanced his way as I laughed. "Natalie?" I said in disbelief as I held her face. "You're awake!"

It looks like their goddess answers human prayers after all.

She nodded slowly—her eyes half-open. "Water," she croaked hoarsely.

Xavier immediately grabbed a water bottle out of his bag and gave it to me.

I pushed my knee up to elevate Natalie's head somewhat for her to drink slowly.

"I'm so fucking glad you're awake," Xavier beamed with a face splitting smile.

Natalie raised her hand to pull the bottle away from her lips, and I screwed the lid back on it before helping her to sit up. She groaned and held her head. I kept holding her arm just in case she fainted.

"I'm sorry," she whispered as she gave me a side glance.

"It's okay. I lived," I replied.

She smiled weakly at me.

"Welcome back," Mathieu interjected.

Natalie held her head up to peer at him in the rear-view mirror. "It's good to be back, Uncle. I'm hungry."

Mathieu frowned. "We didn't pack any food. It'll be dark in another half an hour, and we're already running late."

She sighed. "Please. I feel like there is a crater in my gut. There's a root I must get. It'll help replenish the blood I lost and speed up healing."

"We're in the middle of nowhere right now, Nat," Xavier said. "There is nowhere to get any kind of root."

Natalie looked out the window to find towering trees on either side of the car. "There is," she stated. "Turn left half a mile from here. There's a town. I'll be able to get it there."

Mathieu sighed. "That's going to take us even more off course. But if you really need it…okay, sure. We'll just have to be on high alert, okay?"

Xavier nodded gravely.

Mathieu studied her through the mirror. "So, do you mind telling me what happened back there? What was that scream?"

"I didn't know I could do that either," she replied. She pulled her nightgown away from her body and then gave Xavier a look. "You changed me? It had better not have been Axel."

He rolled his eyes. "I changed you. You were covered in blood."

She swallowed. The look in her eyes was one I knew all too well. It was the same look I had when I'd woken up after being attacked, the memory—the lingering phantom feelings.

She peered down at her wrist. Although only a red mark was visible, her eyes fluttered closed as she pressed a finger against the bruises.

I placed my hand gently over hers.

Pausing, she looked at me, and her eyes welled with tears. I squeezed her hand in support and understanding as she nodded and leaned back. She turned away from me to stare out the window, and I knew it was just to hide her tears. Nevertheless, she continued to hold tightly to my hand. She cautiously asked, "Is Axel—"

"He's alive," I reassured her before she even finished the question. "He went back to his pack."

"And the book?" she questioned.

"It's with us." Mathieu nodded. "Ruby suggested we make a video. Xavier made one that'll be sent to other alphas that might not have come into contact with any vampires yet. Those packs might not have any information on how to deal with the vampires."

She finally turned my way again briefly. "That's a good idea."

"Yeah," I acknowledged as I blushed. "We made it just before we left the house."

Mathieu made the left turn.

I frowned as the tingling sensation I'd been feeling unexpectedly started to make its way up my arm. My body suddenly felt warm, almost like I was getting a fever.

Natalie's head whipped toward me.

I pulled my hand away from Natalie and pretended to

scratch at my chin to distract from the fact that I was purposely trying to move away. I wasn't sure if it was an after effect of what she'd done to me, but I knew I didn't want to ask or say anything about it.

Natalie was already sick. I didn't want to be more of a burden to Xavier and Mathieu, especially right now. The night was fast approaching, and we were about to be caught in it.

"Are you okay?" Natalie asked with concern.

I nodded.

"Are you sure? Are you feeling dizzy or nauseous? I've never done what I just did to you. I don't know what effect it'll have on you or if it'll have any at all."

I gave her my best reassuring smile. "Trust me. I feel okay. My head was hurting earlier, but that's gone now. Honestly, I'm just pretty hungry as well." I placed my hand on my stomach. "I'm starving actually," I told her truthfully.

"We'll stop and grab something to eat. Then we'll get the root you need, Natalie, and find a motel quickly," Mathieu interjected.

"Sure. Trust me. I understand the danger," Natalie said in a low voice as she once again held her wrist.

I was having trouble moving past what had happened to me. I didn't know if I ever would. I wanted to know if only one vampire had bitten Natalie so many times or if there was more to what happened to her. I held my tongue, as I didn't want to make her uncomfortable by bringing up her trauma.

We drove on in silence.

Natalie dozed off eventually, her eyes damp with tears.

Natalie

*T*he vampire sank his fangs into my shoulder and immediately went into a frenzy. His blood lust increased a thousandfold as he started to attack me, only to bite me. After that, he no longer wanted to kill me quickly.

He had won the fight. I'll never forget how he declared, "I've never tasted blood like yours," with such disturbing excitement, as my blood dripped from his sharp white fangs. I lost my strength swiftly after he got the upper hand. That was when he started biting me all over. His mouth was like a vacuum, sucking almost all the blood from my body within minutes.

I guess I had my lineage to blame for that. No doubt, he'd never tasted the blood of a demi-god.

On the brink of death, as my eyes slowly closed, I saw Axel appear behind the vampire and rip his head off with his bare hands.

I owed Axel my life.

Many animals lick their wounds because their saliva has antibacterial and antimicrobial properties. Fortunately for me, the same goes for werewolves. In fact, the effect is even stronger in werewolves than other animals due to their size. Axel acted promptly to find all my wounds and stop the bleeding, then rushed me back to the house. I fell unconscious before we got there, but I did remember whispering Ruby's name to him before that.

He had told me he would find her, and then I lost consciousness.

I felt like I was falling down a bottomless black pit. I could hear everyone talking around me, but my lips wouldn't move as I attempted to scream to them. I eventually stopped screaming and just kept falling. It wasn't a bottomless hole after all, and I ultimately fell into a black sea. There I remained, floating, until I had that vision.

Suddenly, I opened my eyes. I was standing in a small town. I looked around confused before concluding what happened with the vampire and the sea of black must've been just an unusually vivid dream. While enjoying the cold night air, I stopped at a stoplight, waiting for the light to change so I could walk across the crosswalk. Without warning, a man ran up and attacked a woman, ripping her throat out with his hand before pressing his face into the wound.

Vampires started pouring into the busy street—the blood, the screams, the fear, and horror that followed triggered my powers. I wanted to help, I wanted to stop the bloodshed around me, and when I was attacked as well, I just reacted.

I screamed with anger and pain on a level like I'd never done before. The vampire was thrown off me, and I got to my knees as I continued to scream. My eyes closed as I focused on targeting all the vampire minds that I could find.

I wasn't sure how I was doing it, but I tried to kill as many of them as I could before whatever was happening to me faded. Enchanteds didn't have abilities we could use to fight. We performed spells that took time and a lot of preparation. We saw the future, past, and present. We were dream-walkers and, apparently, telepaths from what Reika had taught me.

This was when I felt a warm hand on my cheek and without thinking…I reached out.

Ruby had been pulled into my vision. It had been then when I realized I had a vision, and it wasn't real. Sometimes,

I could tell it was a vision not long after it started, and other times it took a while.

Since I'd woken up, moving even a hand required more energy than it should. Beetroot was what I needed. The IV drip Axel started had worked well, but now I needed more. I couldn't afford to be this weak when we were at risk of being attacked at any moment.

We arrived in the town just as darkness settled and immediately found a diner.

While Xavier and Mathieu ordered our food, Ruby helped me to the bathroom to get changed.

Somewhere, somehow, all those people were going to die.

I kept trying to put a brave face on, but I felt exhausted and petrified. Feeling that vampire sink his fangs into me, again and again, was the second-worst pain I've ever felt. I couldn't escape the memory of it. I sat in the bathroom stall with my hand over my mouth as I cried, and the worst part was—I knew the worst was yet to come.

Ruby

I finished my two sandwiches in record time, and Natalie finished three.

Even though he had eaten four of them himself, Xavier stared at us in disbelief. He told us the waitress inside the diner recommended a motel and had given them directions.

However, Natalie couldn't wait to eat, so we were still parked in the diner's parking lot.

Mathieu remained outside, a beer in hand.

I knew he was upset that we didn't make it back to the others.

It couldn't be helped, unfortunately. Xavier agreed that we had to stop here. It was better to rest in this town for the night, rather than risk driving for who knows how long to get to the next town and then to the pack. A lot could happen quickly and without warning. Xavier didn't want a repeat of what had happened to Axel, him, and me on that highway.

I wasn't interested in being bitten ever again either.

"I'm really sorry about what happened earlier. You weren't supposed to see all of that," Natalie apologized sadly to me.

I shrugged. Of course, I wasn't angry with her. It wasn't her fault. She was unconscious while it was all happening.

"That goes for you and Mathieu, too," she remarked to Xavier.

He waved his hand dismissively.

"You don't need to be sorry," I told her. "We were all there. We know what happened and that it was unintentional."

"Yeah, I still feel bad, though, you know? Why couldn't I have discovered these powers the other night?" She sighed. "Everything happens in its own time, I suppose."

"Doesn't it bother you?" I questioned her. "Seeing visions like that, and you're unable to help, unable to warn anyone."

She nodded and stared out her window at the darkness on the left side of the parking lot. "It's incredibly depressing, but when it's about someone I know, I always tell them or warn them if it's something bad. I don't get visions like…that one often." She glanced back at me and then at Xavier with a small smile on her lips. "If I got visions like that on the regular, I'd lose my mind for sure."

"Sooooo," I drawled. "It was the future then? Or has it already happened? Can you tell?"

"It's the future. Sometimes I can tell by what's in the vision."

"Can you try and remember anything?" I asked. "I've been trying to, but the memory is blurry."

"That's because you weren't meant to see what you saw. You were pulled into it. That's why I was asking you if you were okay. I don't know what effect it'll have on you mentally." Her voice was low as she eyed me up and down with concern.

I felt like wrapping my hands around myself to stop her from seeing through me. "I told you, I feel fine."

Xavier was now eyeing me from the front seat, and that was something I definitely didn't want. I could still feel an odd warmth throughout my body, but other than that, I felt perfectly fine. There was no need for me to mention anything and cause panic. Natalie would only blame herself more. "So, do you remember anything? A sign, the name on a building, anything?"

She bit at her lip and shook her head as a distant look appeared with her eyes. "There's nothing familiar about the town, to be honest. Things like that miss me during visions. Sometimes, I'll be somewhere in the vision I've never been or seen before, but it feels normal to me."

I felt useless and could only imagine how messed up Natalie must have felt. "So, there is no way to prevent it. All those people are going to die?"

"Even if Natalie could pick out something, we can't save an entire town," Xavier interjected.

I stared at him with disbelief. How could he say something like that, and so casually? Innocent lives were going to be taken, and we knew about it.

He stared back at me defiantly. "I'm still healing, and Natalie can barely walk on her own. It's just you, me, and Dad. He's the only one out of all of us that's at full strength. We can't go looking for trouble right now based on a glimpse of a future that might change."

I bit down on my lip. As much as I wanted to argue with him, I knew he had a point.

Natalie bumped me with her elbow. "He's right, you know. Sometimes, I get glimpses of the future, but it's only one possible outcome. Anything or everything might change."

I supposed I would have to live with that. I'd always been a loner, and frankly, most humans annoy me. However, I was still a human, so I couldn't stand by and watch my race get turned into snack food for vampires or any other supernatural. Now that I knew about werewolves and the supernatural world, I was completely ready and willing to be a part of it.

Of course, I couldn't exactly be on the front lines, but I would find my place. I looked over at Xavier. For now, just being a Luna would have to do. As Luna, I guess I would at least have a say in decisions about the pack.

"Xavier, what do you think we'd all be doing right now if we were all still just normal college students?" Natalie asked.

I laughed.

"She said *normal*," I teased.

Xavier laughed while she elbowed me.

I sobered up. "I'd be doing overtime at the diner right now."

"I'd be working out right now," Xavier said almost yearningly.

I rolled my eyes. Of course, he'd say something like that. I shook my head and rolled my eyes.

He glanced at me. "What? I'm losing my abs."

"There are more important things in life than your abs, Xavier." I scoffed.

He lifted his shirt.

I tried not to react. *What the fuck does he mean by he's losing his abs?* Even sitting down, I could clearly make out his perfectly chiseled six-pack.

Natalie leaned over to me. "He just wanted to lift his shirt."

He flashed me a wide grin.

Natalie chuckled as she held her chin thoughtfully. "I'd be hooking up with someone."

My mouth fell open at this.

Xavier's face twisted with disgust. "Jesus, Natalie, I really didn't need to hear that."

Natalie laughed.

Xavier and I glanced at each other for a second because it was the first time we had heard a genuine laugh from her in a long time. She'd always been the one to set the mood and make everyone happy. Without her, this bleak world just seemed much more so.

"What?" She chuckled. "It's the truth." She started coughing really loudly.

I quickly gave her the rest of my water.

"I'm okay," she said once she stopped coughing. "I'm fine." She gave the water bottle back to me and paused as she stared at me.

I took it from her. *There is that look again—why does she keep staring at me like that?* "Um, what?" I asked.

She shook her head. "It's nothing. Sorry. I just thought I saw something."

I raised a brow. "Uh, okay, then."

Mathieu opened the driver's door and was about to climb into the car when we heard a scream. People started pouring out of the diner.

My heart began hammering in my chest.

Natalie grabbed my arm, her nails digging into my skin. She held her head up and began inhaling deeply. Her hold on me soon relaxed. "There aren't any vampires. I don't smell anything."

"Me neither," Xavier added as he got out of the car.

Despite the lack of vampire scent, people were continuing to rush out of the diner. My interest was piqued. I hopped out of the car as well, and Natalie followed behind me as we all stood by the car to watch people leave one right after the other.

They all seemed to be in a panic. A horrible feeling settled on my chest.

"What's got their panties in a twist?" Natalie asked with confusion.

I shrugged.

"I'll go check it out," Xavier volunteered as he moved away.

I quickly followed him.

"You should stay in the car."

I snorted and kept walking. "Not a chance."

A man rushed out the door and hopped into his car before speeding off.

"Seriously, what's going on?" I wondered aloud.

We entered the diner to see a few people bundled up at the counter with their heads back as they stared up at the television. I looked around the rest of the restaurant. Sure enough, all the seats were empty.

A woman hurried by me, and I gently tapped her shoulder. Her wide brown and teary eyes met mine, and I frowned. "Um, what's going on?"

She pointed to the television and rushed out the door, pulling her daughter unceremoniously behind her. I watched her through the transparent door as she picked up the little girl and started running.

The fuck?

"Ruby," Xavier called to me.

I turned to look at him.

He too was now staring at the television. "Look."

The reporter on the news show was a woman with short black hair to her shoulders. "I must warn you, the video that is about to be shown is quite graphic."

My eyes widened as I read the headline.

Vampire sighting caught on camera.

Fuck! I looked over at Xavier.

He stared back at me, and his jaw clenched.

Heavy breathing could be heard coming from the television, and I peered up to see a shaky recording of what appeared to be a man hunched over another person.

The video was being shot through what looked like an

iron fence. Judging from all the flowers and trees, I guessed this must have been made in a park.

It was night time, and coupled with the clearly nervous and shaky hand, it was a little hard to see what was happening. The person suddenly stopped shaking as the man that was hunched over sat up.

My eyes widened as blood dripped from the man's abnormally wide mouth, the lamp above them offering some light to see him by. The people around us started to gasp, and more of them began to leave as the man's tongue darted out to lick his lips.

His fangs could not be missed as he stretched his mouth wide once more and fell forward onto the body beneath him, continuing with his meal.

"This can't be real!" a man suddenly yelled. "This has to be some kind of prank!"

The person holding the phone sobbed, and my heart fell as the vampire looked up. His red eyes caught the woman instantly, and within seconds, he was rushing towards her.

I closed my eyes as the woman screams mixed with inhuman growls and hissing, then the video ended.

The reporter returned to the screen, clearly shaken up as well. "The victim's body was found in the park two days after this video was taken, along with the first victim's mutilated body. Both bodies were completely drained of blood. This grisly finding matches several other murders that have been taking place all over the country in the past couple of days."

I stopped listening. My fear—our fear of the humans finding out about the vampires was actually materializing before our eyes. As I looked around at the terrified faces, I started to panic as well but for an entirely different reason. If vampires were now confirmed to be real, they would have no further reason to hide.

The reporter continued speaking, warning people to take this threat seriously, stay indoors during the night, and not to travel alone.

"This is bad. This is really bad," Xavier muttered under his breath. "I knew this shit was going to happen."

The rest of the people in the diner started to leave, even the man who'd been skeptical.

"Hey, I'm sorry, but we're closing," a waitress said to us. She laughed nervously. "Just in case this isn't some prank, you know?"

Xavier smiled at her, but the smile didn't reach his eyes. "I understand." He turned to face me. "Let's go."

As he placed his hand on my shoulder, I winced and bent forward.

He paused. "Hey, are you okay?"

I paused and let out a breath as I tried not to show how afraid I felt. The pain had shot through my arm when Xavier touched me. Then it faded as quickly as it had come. "A cramp," I lied. "Must be those sandwiches I had."

"Come on, the sooner we find a motel, the better. I think Natalie's going to have to go without that root tonight."

We were almost at the door when a loud explosion rattled the glass windows. We hunched down as we started looking around. Then Xavier rushed outside. I was right on his heels as we ran back to the car. When we turned around, black smoke was bubbling to the sky in the distance.

"It came from the town," Mathieu informed us. "What's going on?"

"Someone took a video of a vampire feeding," I told him. "It's all over the news."

He clenched his fists, his eyes turning black as he rounded the car and pulled the door open. "We need to go. Now!"

Natalie started coughing, harder than before, and as she pulled her hand away from her mouth, her palm was coated with blood. "I can't leave without that root," she said shakily as she fell onto the car.

Xavier started sniffling loudly beside me.

I didn't have to ask what he smelled. I could smell it too, the pungent scent that followed vampires like the rain clouds that appear before a storm.

He grabbed my arm as Natalie climbed into the car. "We have to get the root for her and get the hell out of here," he insisted as he looked at his father.

Mathieu's eyes were still as black as the sky above us.

Natalie started coughing again, and more blood began to spill from her mouth. She was beginning to look pale all over again.

"We have to get it, Dad. She needs it."

"Natalie, why is this happening?" I asked her, my hands shaking by my side. Not from the sight of her blood or the fact I could smell those disgusting vampires, but because of the pulsating heat under my skin.

"The power I used," she said breathlessly. "My body isn't reacting well to it, that's all."

Xavier hissed. "That's all? You're coughing up blood. You look like you're about to pass out!" He closed her car door with more force than he needed. "Tell me where to get that root, so we can get the hell out of here."

10

XAVIER

*M*y worst fears were becoming a reality before my very eyes. I believed it would only be a matter of time before the humans found out vampires were the ones committing the recent murders. I had just hoped it wouldn't come to that.

If they found out vampires were real, which they now had, they would start to wonder what other supernatural creatures might be real. This was a total fucking disaster. For decades, these bloodsuckers remained in hiding, no doubt feeding just the same. Now suddenly, one slipped up.

If he realized he was being recorded, why had the vampire left the phone behind for someone to find?

I'd hoped this war they'd started would remain in the shadows of our dark world, but I had been foolish to think so.

In a matter of days, they'd sent the wolf community into a panic. Now they revealed the existence of supernaturals to humans. I might be mated to a human, but that didn't stop me from admitting the truth about them—some humans were too fragile to deal with the existence of supernaturals. Or should I say the majority of them?

Despite how we'd met, Ruby hadn't completely lost her shit at the discovery of werewolves. What she experienced at the hand of that vampire had been another horrible experience for her. And of course, her life was still in danger from the Council. She was being hit on all sides, but she was still standing. In fact, she wanted to go looking for vampires. She wanted to fight. Many wolves wouldn't want to help the way she did, and I felt proud to call her my mate.

Humans were many things, but one thing was certain— they were resilient. History had proven that they could be dangerous enemies, even for supernaturals. The humans would react to this vampire threat quickly. Whether or not they succeeded in containing the vampire threat, the world around us was in for a deadly roller coaster ride while they tried.

"Did you find anything?" Dad asked Natalie, who was scrolling through the internet on her phone.

She nodded and held the phone up to show me a picture of a witch's shop. "She's the real deal. She'll have what I need."

The faster we left, the better, but I didn't want Natalie to suffer any more than she already had. She was still healing from the attack. Then she placed even more pressure on her body by using powers she'd never used before and didn't know how to control. I committed the picture to memory and was about to walk off.

Then Dad spoke, "Are you sure this root will help you, and it's all you need? Can't we find it once we get to the pack?"

Her shoulders rose and fell slowly as she shrugged. "Maybe, but once we leave this town and get to the pack...no one will be allowed to leave. I feel like I'm dying, Uncle. I need that root now while I'm sure I can get it."

"Dad, I'll be quick, okay." I understood his need to get the hell out of this place, but putting Natalie at risk of getting worse overnight wasn't something I was prepared to do. "I can smell it too, but the scent isn't so strong yet. There must not be a lot of them here."

"I doubt there needs to be a lot of them to create chaos," he pointed out.

Just then, another thundering boom echoed around us. The street lamps and the lights in the diner went out.

Ruby's heartbeat increased, and I took her hand to reassure her. She looked up at me, and despite the darkness around us, I could see her just fine. Her pupils were dilated to allow her to see a little better in the dark. I could hear frantic running and a chorus of voices coming from the town, and the lights came back on. "I'll find the witch's shop and be right back."

Ruby held onto my wrist. "I'm coming with you."

I shook my head no. "It's best if you stay here, Ruby."

"I'm coming with you, Xavier. I might not be much backup, but you can't go alone." She inhaled through her nose. "Besides, I don't smell vampires anymore. Can you still smell them?"

I took in the air, and sure enough, the scent was gone. According to what Axel had said, humans couldn't smell the stench emanating from vampires. So how could Ruby smell them? Maybe that bit of detail was wrong?

Those were questions for another time. With whatever

vampires in town now gone, I felt a little more at ease. "I can hear what's happening in town right now, and you being there is a bad idea. The humans are looting. They're panicking, and I can't say I blame them."

"Guys," Natalie called to us weakly.

Ruby walked away, clearly determined. "We're going."

I sighed and hurried to catch up to her.

She nodded. "It's only humans running around right now, and I have a werewolf with me. I think I'll be fine. Let's find this shop so that we can get out of here. Things are going to get really bad really fast."

"I know. We're going to have to leave before dawn to avoid the traffic. Trust me, there will be traffic."

Ruby sighed as she shoved her hands into the pockets of her jacket. "If only these people understood there's nowhere they can hide."

Ruby

*N*ews of the existence of vampires had sent the world into chaos in a matter of minutes. People were looting shops and supermarkets before rushing home to hide.

Xavier kept me close to his side as we walked through the noisy street. People were running with things they'd looted falling out of their hands. Sirens were blazing as cops tried to gain control over the madness, and fire trucks were already on site to put out the already numerous fires.

I wonder if this is what it's like all over the world right now?

"Hey, what happened with the lights just now?" Xavier asked a man who was about to run past us.

His dark hair tousled, and his glasses rested on the tip of his nose. "Someone tried to blow up the power station transformer. Look, you two need to get inside!" A car's tires screeched, startling the man. He jumped a mile and scurried off.

Xavier held my hand as we raced through the crowds. The stench of smoke hung thick in the air, making my nose burn a little as I watched two women fight for a television. I shook my head in dismay.

Instead of trying to get food, people were breaking into stores for expensive clothes and appliances. They wouldn't have any use for any of that if the vampires attacked. What would they do when they were trapped inside their homes with no food, but they still had a brand-new television or a Gucci outfit? I'd rather have food and a gun over what these people were rolling on the ground and fighting for.

I frowned and squeezed Xavier's hand as I was hit with a wave of nausea. Maybe I needed some of that beetroot that Natalie wanted us to get. Whatever was happening to me started after she showed me her vision. Maybe it was an after effect.

No, if I was honest, I'd been feeling different ever since that vampire attacked me. For a while, I'd worried I was changing into one. I'd felt horrible on the inside, but the feeling had faded, only to return the night they attacked the Blackmoon house.

Being exposed to Natalie's magic made me feel so much worse.

Why the fuck am I sweating so much?

"Hey." Xavier paused to cup my cheek. "Are you okay, Ruby?"

I nodded more confidently than I felt. "Yeah, yeah, I'm just wondering where the hell this shop is." Someone threw a bottle into a window across the street. "Xavier." I tapped his shoulder rapidly with a smile before pointing to the shop next to the store that was being broken into. "There it is. That's it, right?"

Looking relieved to finally find the shop, he took my hand again as we ran across the street. Twice already, we'd seen people almost get hit by cars. The world around us was starting to look more and more like a war zone.

"You'd think all these people would head straight home," I noted. "None of them seem to realize they're all in the open to be picked off if vamps attack now."

Xavier went up the steps of the tiny store, his hand still holding mine. He was so cute. If I wasn't pressed to his side or if he wasn't holding my hand, he'd lose his shit. He tapped a finger against the open sign and looked back at me. "I guess it's business as usual here, huh?" He opened the door and stepped in.

As I followed him in, my nostrils filled with the heady scent of incense. The shelves upon shelves of books reminded me of the library at my college. I'd expected a shop filled with strange objects and artifacts, not a book shop. My eyes fell on a woman at the back of the room behind and counter.

She didn't look up at us and continued to skim through a magazine casually.

"Hello, aren't you worried about what's going on outside?

Someone might break-in," I said to her.

Looking up at us, she smiled. She placed her elbow on the counter beside the magazine and rested her cheek in her hand, "I see no point in panicking. There's a spell on the door to repel anyone with bad intentions. You two made it in, so I guess I'm safe."

"So, you're the witch then?" Xavier asked.

She stood up straight. She looked like a normal woman with slightly greying hair and warm eyes with glasses resting on her nose. "That's me," she replied with a smile.

"What if a vampire tries to break in? Is your spell strong enough to keep them out?" I asked.

She shook her head. "No, but I do have my own ways of getting out of a sticky situation." She closed the magazine. "So, how may I help you?"

"Do you have beetroot? An Enchanted was attacked by vampires."

She raised a brow as she looked from Xavier to me and paused.

I stared at her in confusion as to why she was suddenly staring at me.

She looked me up and down and then tilted her head to the side.

Considering how bad I was feeling after sharing Natalie's vision and the terrible after effects, if that's what they were, I wasn't in the mood to be scrutinized by some strange witch. I lost it and snapped, "Excuse me, is there a problem?"

She narrowed her eyes at me. "What are you?"

I knew this woman wasn't blind. Considering she was a witch, she should be able to tell what I was, shouldn't she? "I'm human," I answered in a low voice.

She made clicking sounds with her tongue as she held her chin.

I looked over at Xavier, who glanced at me before turning his watchful eyes back at the witch.

"Yes, I can see that you're human…" She wagged her finger at me. "But there is something more inside you. Perhaps you are just ill. Your aura is not stable. It's changing colors quite rapidly."

Whatever that means! I suppose that explains why Natalie kept looking at me strangely. "Well," I drawled. "I'm only human. I'm just not feeling well."

Xavier turned to face me, his anger evident by the look on his face.

I braced myself for a cussing.

"What?" he demanded. "Since when? Why haven't you said anything, Ruby?"

"Since the incident with Nat in the car. I didn't say anything because, um…" I pointed to the door. "You have enough to worry about along with Natalie. She's worse than I am. I just feel a little hot and uncomfortable sometimes."

"Ruby, Natalie asked you if you were okay. We don't know how you might have been affected by what happened." He glared. "Are you sure that's all you're feeling?"

"Yes, just a little hot sometimes." I turned to the witch. "Do you have beetroot or not?"

"Sure, I do, but she'll need a little lime juice extract as well. Give me a minute." She disappeared into the back.

I looked over at Xavier to find him staring daggers at me. "I am fine, Xavier. I'll have some of the beetroots as well, okay?" He said nothing but continued to stare at me, and I sighed. "Relax. Natalie is the priority right now."

The witch returned with a brown paper bag and handed it to Xavier. "She has to crush the beetroot with the skin and all, then add the lime juice."

Xavier took the bag from her and pulled out his wallet to pay.

She held up her hand. "It's on the house."

"Um, thank you," he replied.

She shrugged then nodded her head towards the door. "Hard times are coming," she cautioned as she sighed heavily. "I can hop to another world, but for you folks, you all..."

"I'm sorry, what?" I asked. *Did she just say she could hop to another world?* I knew I shouldn't have been surprised, but I couldn't help it.

She smiled at me like a person would at a child who'd said something adorable. She probably figured out I was new to this world. "It comes with a price, of course. There is always a price to be paid. Your Enchanted friend is now paying the price from using magic she shouldn't be able to." She pursed her lips. "To have done it to begin with, she must be strong, whatever she did." While speaking, she focused on me, a strange expression on her face again. This time, her eyes slowly began to turn violet.

"Okay, thanks for everything," Xavier told her and turned to leave.

"Wait." She held her hand out to me. "Let me see your palm."

I made a face. "Um, why?" I felt unnerved. Willow hadn't been this creepy.

"I don't bite. Let me see your palm."

I looked at Xavier to gauge his reaction. He didn't seem too bothered by her request, so I gave her my hand.

She closed her eyes as her hand hovered over mine. A few seconds passed with me growing more and more impatient before her eyes popped open. "You're mated to him," she suddenly declared, and her violet eyes widened with shock as she looked at Xavier.

He grew tense, and I pulled my hand away from her.

"How is that even possible?" Her eyes began to glow even brighter. "How are you mated to two wolves? You're human."

Xavier grabbed my hand, "Thanks for your help, but that's none of your business. Ruby, let's go."

Her shocked and curious eyes returned to me.

Xavier started pulling me to the door when he halted.

I looked him up and down, wondering why he stopped, when suddenly—I smelled it.

"Vampires," he said under his breath.

I hunched forward as white-hot pain began to roll through my body. The scent of vampires started to grow stronger, making me feel as if I was about to throw up. I staggered away from Xavier.

He held onto me to stop me from falling over. "Ruby? Ruby, what's wrong?"

"I can smell them. I feel sick," I replied as the pain started to subside, but now there was a heaviness on my chest. I stood up straight. My eyes closed as I breathed in and out through my mouth. "It's like I keep getting hot flashes."

"What's wrong with her?" Xavier demanded as he turned to the witch. He called her forward, "What can you see?"

"Something is wrong with her, but I can't tell what. The way her aura is shifting colors like that means her entire being is off balance. That's why I thought she was sick." The witch explained in a low voice as she drew closer to us. She placed her hand firmly on my forehead. "I can't tell why this is happening. Maybe it has to do with her being mated to you and whoever else, but she's reacting to something." The pain dulled to the point where it was at least bearable. "I've never seen anything like this before," she whispered in awe. "No wonder you seemed more than human."

"How can I seem more than human? Yes, I'm mated to wolves, but I'm not a wolf myself. What else is there to make me seem not one hundred percent human?" I was getting angry. How could she say something like that? Reika or Natalie would have sensed if I had any other form of supernatural blood, right?

"I don't know," she replied with uncertainty.

I sighed with frustration as I pinched the bridge of my nose.

She went on, "I've never seen this before. And how can you smell vampires? I thought humans couldn't." She turned to Xavier angrily. "Just who are you people anyway?"

First, it was the barrier in my mind, and now I'm...sick? Changing? I don't even know!

She sighed. "Nevermind. Just keep an eye on her, or you will lose her. If she doesn't die from whatever is happening to her, she will still be at risk from others, wolves especially, if they learn about this."

Too late, I wanted to scream.

Xavier nodded, took my hand, and we left hastily.

With the scent of the vampires growing stronger, we knew we needed to move quickly. The first time we scented them, it might have been only one, but the odor was much stronger now. There had to be a lot of them. "Call Mathieu and see if they're okay. Tell them we're on our way back so they know we're coming," I suggested.

Xavier nodded and pulled out the extra phone Mathieu had given us. I'd lost mine and hadn't had a chance to replace it yet. No one called me anyways, but maybe it was time for us to get new ones for situations like these.

"Dad, we're coming back. We got the beetroot." He paused as he listened. "Yeah, we smell them. We're coming." He ended the call just as a piercing scream rang through the night.

My heart skipped a beat with fright as I spun around. My hand started to shake because I knew that was a woman being attacked by a vampire. I felt it in my bones. With all the looting and chaos, no one would give a second thought to someone screaming.

Another scream rang out—then another.

I didn't think about it, and I didn't give my legs the command to move. Yet before I knew it, I was running in the direction of the scream. It was as if my body was moving of its own accord or I was being pulled by something.

All I knew was I needed to get to this woman. I had no idea what I'd do when I got there, but I pulled my dagger out and kept moving.

At first, Xavier yelled for me to come back, but he soon ran after me after he realized I had no intention of stopping. Of course, with his long legs and powerful legs, he caught up to me fairly quickly. As he wrapped his hands around my waist, another blood-curdling scream resonated through the night air, and frightened people started running past us. He lowered me to the ground and moved to stand before me. "I can't shift. There are too many people here."

I stepped out from behind him and walked forward as if in a trance. I turned in a circle as screaming men and women ran past me. The vision I had seen so long ago during the mind link with Reika and Natalie resurfaced.

My blood chilled in my veins, and I started running against the crowd. Xavier's hands wrapped around my wrist to pull me back, but I yanked my hand away. "This is it, Xavier!" I screamed in panic.

He stared at me as if I had grown three heads.

I knew I must look crazy to him. At this moment, I felt crazy, but this was what I had seen. "This is the vision I saw with Reika and Natalie." I pointed behind me. "I ran that way in the vision, so I need to do the same now. Those shadows were vampires. Why would *I* get a vision about vampires from so long ago?"

His brows pulled together. "I don't know. Are you sure this is the same place?"

"Xavier, I swear it. This is the town I saw in my vision."

He gazed past me, and his eyes narrowed. I looked behind me, but he quickly grabbed my shoulder and turned me back to him. "We need to go now." The words had barely left his lips when a woman behind me started screaming.

I spun around on my heels, startled by the sudden scream, only to see a vampire tackle a blonde woman to the ground. With all the lights, I could easily see his sharp fangs sink into her shoulder and my face twisted as he easily broke her neck.

I fell forward, a scream almost leaving my lips as the ground rushed up to meet me. I held my hands out so I wouldn't fall on my face, and my dagger fell to the side. Growls and hisses reached my ears as I flipped onto my back to see Xavier and a vampire tumbling on the ground in an intense battle.

Despite the street now being deserted by all humans, Xavier couldn't shift in the middle of town. The risk was just too high, especially at a time like this. Confirmation of the existence of werewolves on the same night as vampires would be too much for the human world to handle. Look at how badly they'd behaved already. There were cameras everywhere these days, and the werewolf community being exposed by Xavier was something neither of us wanted. Olcan was already out to get the Blackmoon Pack after what we had done.

Xavier had shifted only his claws as his sole form of defense available against the vampire. He kicked the vampire off him and jumped onto his feet. He stood in a fighting stance and remained still.

The vampire hissed at him and then lunged forward. He recoiled as Xavier swiped at his chest, ripping the black T-shirt he was wearing to shreds.

A young woman ran out from behind a car. The vampire immediately attacked.

My stomach turned as the vampire grabbed her. He turned her to face me and bit rapidly into her throat, before pulling away and ripping her throat wide open. My lips started to quiver as he released her, and she fell to the ground with her hand outstretched to me.

Her hazel eyes fluttered closed within seconds, and the soulless vampire kneeled to finish his meal.

Monsters! Fucking monsters!

I knew the bloodsucking bastard could see me clear as day. He just didn't care. He obviously saw us as nothing more than food. I knew I would be his next meal after he drained that young woman. He didn't even seem to care about his fellow vampire enough to bother to help him out in the fight with Xavier. I could be grateful for that, at least.

The heaviness on my chest grew worse, but I ignored it as I got to my feet. I took a step forward and then another as a tingling sensation took over my body. I was so angry. The world around me started to fade away. Only the vampire remained.

Until today, the young woman beneath him had her whole life ahead of her. Maybe she had a family, kids, a job she loved. Now she was nothing but vampire food, a lifeless corpse being drained in the street. I remembered vividly how deeply violating it felt to be fed on like this. I'd almost died, just like this girl. My body began to shake with a rage I'd never felt before. I wanted to kill this vampire with my bare hands, and the desire to do so was only growing by the second.

The vamp abruptly stopped feeding and pulled back from the woman before glancing to the side. He looked as if he was smelling the air for something. All of a sudden, he turned his head my way and smiled widely with anticipation.

I stared at his red-stained fangs in disgust as blood oozed from his lips.

He wiped his hand across his mouth and patted the woman beneath him. "Thanks, love," he chuckled as he slowly stood to his feet.

Behind us, the growls and hisses from Xavier and the other vampire continued. However, my complete focus was directed on this guy, this creature, this blood-sucking parasite!

The vamp tilted his head to the side.

I did the same.

He smiled in amusement, and it soon turned into thundering laughter. "You're either incredibly brave or very stupid. Since you're human, I'll assume stupid." He looked closer at me. "I must say, you have a rather odd scent. I can't tell if it's your natural body odor or perfume."

I didn't respond, and he stood there waiting to see if I'd reply.

He then shrugged uncaringly, "Whatever it is…has anyone ever told you that you smell deliciously edible?"

I'll just ignore that and the disgusting wink he just sent my way. "Why are you here?" I asked.

His amused expression fell away as if he was caught off guard by my question. He waved his hand to the woman's body by his feet before combing his bloody fingers through his dark hair. "I was eating. What does it look like?"

"Why. Are. You. Here?" I demanded again and this time, stressing each word. "You people haven't been around for forever, so where have you all been?"

He raised a brow and appeared somewhat surprised. Of course, he wouldn't expect an average human to know something like this. "Well, you're an interesting one. What's your name?"

Is this man serious? "Why are you doing this? Why now?" I persisted.

He sighed. "I'm doing this because I can and because *we can*. We're taking back this world. My kind, we're apex predators, and we always have been. We've hidden and lived like rats long enough." He held his arms out wide. "We've waited and waited and waited some more. Now, finally, we can step into the light." His arms fell, and he made a face. "Well, into the light figuratively, of course."

"You're not a predator." I held my right arm and tried not to grimace from the pain. Xavier and the other vampire had moved from where they were before, but I could still hear them fighting. I needed to keep this vampire occupied. If he decided to attack while Xavier was fighting another vamp, I would be as good as dead.

Whatever was happening to me couldn't have picked a worse time. I rarely got sick, but I hadn't felt like myself since that vampire bit me. Like Natalie, I'd received a vision that could have helped to prevent all of this. If I had known the shadows were vampires, I would have told Mathieu. He would have informed the rest of the alphas, and they would've hunted the vampires before they had time to cause all of this trouble. Maybe we could have prevented this from ever happening.

Thinking about that now wouldn't help anything. I hadn't known the shadows were vampires, and I hadn't told Mathieu. Thinking of the past and what-ifs wouldn't stop this vampire from attacking and killing now.

"All of you are pests," I muttered under my breath. I knew he could hear me clearly; his furrowed brows made that clear enough. "You're just monsters and savages. Look at what you've caused in a matter of days. If you plan to take over the world, why are you setting out to destroy it? That's what will happen. That leaves your people with more shit to clean up in the end, but hey, you all won't have to worry about that because it'll never get to that."

"And who is going to stop us?" he bit back. "You?" he asked through clenched teeth. "I admire how brave you are, but it'll only make me enjoy killing you more. Don't act like you humans haven't been destroying this world for decades!" He shoved his hands into his pockets and stepped over the woman's body. "You kill animals to eat them for sustenance, and we vampires do the same. It's how we survive, and we can't help that. Like every living thing, don't we deserve the right to live?"

Well, I guess that settled the argument of whether vampires were capable of rational thought.

"You all should have stayed in hiding," I told him.

His expression filled with fury.

"You're only able to feed on blood to survive. I understand that, but there is a right and wrong way to do that. You know doing all of this is the wrong way, but the thing is, you and your kind like it. Don't you? You do. That woman just now didn't have to die like that. You speak to me as if you are in control of your hunger." I touched my neck. "You don't have to attack humans as if we can't feel it!"

"Ohhhhh," he drawled. "I get it. You were bitten, huh? I can see it." He then tilted his head to the side. "Now I'm curious how you survived." He looked me up and down as he eyed me with suspicion. "Who are you? What makes you think you can stand here and talk to me like this?"

I shrugged. "I thought we were having a peaceful chat."

He started laughing, all the while nodding his head. "I like you. I do. We do have pets, so maybe I'll make you mine." He sighed. "You know, our bite isn't always painful. Whoever attacked you was a fool. He or she should have turned you. Maybe they were just too weak since you're here and I assume they are no longer living." He held a finger up. "But I digress. Anyways, I can be gentle. You don't have to be on the losing side of this, human. Humans, were-wolves, or any other creature on this planet won't be able to beat us this time. I promise you that. If you have no problem hanging out with a werewolf, why can't you join us? Werewolves are just as savage as we are. Maybe even more so."

"You've got to be kidding, right? You hunt humans for food. Werewolves protect the humans."

He snorted and shook his head.

"Maybe not all wolves," I acknowledged. "But you vamps can't compare to wolves, so don't even try." I realized I could no longer hear Xavier and the vampire fighting, and my heart skipped a beat.

The corner of his mouth lifted into a smile as he looked at my chest. "You just realized your little friend went silent, huh?" He clapped his hands. "Well, it was truly nice speaking with you, human girl. I love the red hair, by the way. Did I tell you red is my favorite color? I'll ask you once more...join me. Humans are the real pests and parasites of this world. I won't hold it against you that you were born one, but be smarter and accept my proposal. You'll be treated well. You will only be fed on by me, and I'm gentle." He looked at the woman he'd killed and smiled awkwardly. "Well, most of the time, I'm gentle. You'll survive, child. Be smart about—"

"Fuck you!" I screamed. "One of your kind already showed me what your kind is when he ripped into my throat! Take your proposal and shove it up your walking dead ass!" I saw red. His stench and his sick reasoning finally pushed me to the edge. My body started visibly shaking as if I'd been stuck in the cold for days. An ache I couldn't explain began to build inside me.

"Rafael? Where is Malik?" A man's voice asked from behind me.

I spun around.

It was another vampire. His green eyes drifted to me, and he pointed his thumb in my direction. "What are you waiting for? Kill her, so we can go looking for Navia."

Rafael pointed to his right. "He went that way with the wolf. I'm not in a rush. I like this one."

The man looked at me, and his brows knitted. "What's to like other than her scent? Don't forget we have orders, Rafael. If you won't kill her, I will."

It all happened so quickly. His green eyes turned blood red, and he ran at me, his white fangs elongating as he drew closer.

I just reacted. I opened the door to all the pain, anger, and frustration I've been subjected to and screamed as I raised my hand in an attempt to shield myself.

The vampire halted abruptly, frozen mid-attack. With my heart pounding in my ears, I lowered my hand somewhat.

He stared down at his hand.

I did the same as I frowned when red bumps started to appear on his skin.

I jumped as he started to scream agonizingly, and before my very eyes, his skin began to bubble like boiling water. His pale skin began to turn red, and my eyes widened. I stepped back as he appeared to be burning from the inside out.

What the fuck? D-did I just do that?

His skin began to blacken and char, and he fell to his knees. I winced as I heard his bones break, and he turned his head to the side. "Rafael!" he screamed as he fell forward and smoke began to rise from his body.

I swallowed and looked down at my hand uncertainly. My palm was bright red and shaking. My lips parted as I began to breathe slowly.

What is happening to me? I-I killed him. Did I just kill him?

"How did you do that?" Rafael asked, shock evident in his voice.

My head snapped towards him.

"How the fuck did you do that?" he yelled.

Black lines were now making their way from his neck to the base of his mouth. He looked both pissed and confused as he gazed from me to the dead vampire. He crouched down low and hissed at me.

I started to step back.

A loud crash echoed around us, drawing our attention, and I came face to face with Xavier.

He had thrown the vampire he had been fighting into a car's windshield. His eyes were black, and his claws were dripping with blood. He paused as he quickly looked from me to Rafael then to the dead vampire on the ground.

"Pay attention!" Rafael roared.

I spun around to find him inches away from me, causing me to fall backward on my ass. I closed my eyes as Xavier yelled, "No!" I held my hands up to shield my face. This time, I could feel heat coursing through my hands down to my palm, and then there was silence.

A gurgling sound made me open my eyes. I gasped and crawled back on my hands.

Rafael's face was turning from pale to red to a dark burnt shade. He wasn't screaming like the other one did, but his eyes were wide with shock. He then fell to the ground.

I looked away as one of his crisp charred arms broke off

his body. I sat up and stared at my hands as the redness from my palms traveled further up my arms. Tears began to sting my eyes.

Xavier rushed over to me.

Behind him, the vampire he'd been fighting fell off the car and gaped at me as if I was the monster. In the blink of an eye, he was gone.

"Ruby! Ruby?"

I could hear Xavier clearly, but I couldn't speak, not with the burning in my hands.

"What the fuck just happened? Ruby?"

Tears began to roll down my cheeks, but they felt hot on my skin. I held my shaky hands out to him, my breathing now shallow, as I started to feel weak. I didn't know what just happened or how it happened, but whatever it was—it was backfiring on me.

"Hot, I'm hot," I forced out as my head rolled to the side.

Xavier quickly grabbed me. "No, no, no. Fuck! Stay awake, okay?"

Though my eyes were mere slits by now, I could still see the panic in his eyes. More tears ran like little rivers down my cheeks.

"Fuck!" He howled loud, long, and hard before looking back down at me. "Come on, baby, don't do this to me. Stay awake!"

"Something's inside me, Xavier." I started sobbing feebly. I felt so weak, I could barely move. The fire burning under my skin raged on. "It's burning me. It's burning me alive!"

The world around me went black.

THE LUNA RISING UNIVERSE
CONTINUES...

LUNA DARKNESS

Luna Darkness (Book 4)

https://ssbks.com/LR4

With a war raging between vampires, humans, and werewolves...

...the world has been thrown into a state of *CHAOS*.

Humans are selfish creatures that believe the world belongs to them and only them.

Despite the fact that werewolves hate vampires and want them gone as much as the humans do, they are being hunted along with the vampires.

I didn't know what was happening when I *single-handedly* killed two vampires when they attacked me.

It released something hidden deep within me, and now I'm wanted by vampires, werewolves, and humans.

I'm a freak among freaks.

Now I'm the hunted among the hunted, running for my life with my knights by my side, my two alphas, Xavier and Axel.

But what the hell is happening to me?!

Everything is changing.

The world is coming to an end.

https://ssbks.com/LR4

THE BLOODMOON WARS (A PARANORMAL SHIFTER SERIES PREQUEL TO LUNA RISING)

The Awakening (Book 1)

https://ssbks.com/BW1

The Enlightenment (Book 2)

https://ssbks.com/BW2

The Revolution(Book 3)

https://ssbks.com/BW3

The Renaissance (Book 4)

https://ssbks.com/BW4

The Dawn (Book 5)

https://ssbks.com/BW5

THE VENANDI UNIVERSE

THE VENANDI CHRONICLES

Demon Marked (Book 1)

https://ssbks.com/VC1

Demon Kiss (Book 2)

https://ssbks.com/VC2

Demon Huntress (Book 3)

https://ssbks.com/VC3

Demon Desire (Book 4)

https://ssbks.com/VC4

Demon Eternal (Book 5)

https://ssbks.com/VC5

THE DESTINE UNIVERSE

DESTINE ACADEMY SERIES (A MAGICAL
ACADEMY SERIES)

Destine Academy Books 1-10 Boxed Set

https://ssbks.com/DA1-10

HAVE YOU READ THE LUNA RISING PREQUEL?

Click below to get your FREE copy of the **Luna Rising Prequel**.

https://ssbks.com/LunaPrequel

Axel

I'm next in line to be **ALPHA**

…and I'm ready for the challenge.

Focused and determined to make my father proud, I won't let *anything* get in my way.

Until the day I met **HER...**

She's a drop-dead <u>gorgeous</u> blonde with eyes like an aquamarine gem...and she's a witch.

But I'm a werewolf.

And some unions are **FORBIDDEN...**

That little witch has turned my world upside down.

All love comes at a cost.

But this love may cost me *everything...*

https://ssbks.com/LunaPrequel

ENJOY THIS BOOK? I WOULD LOVE TO HEAR FROM YOU...

Thank you very much for downloading my eBook. I hope you enjoyed reading it as much as I did writing it!

Reviews of my books are an incredibly valuable tool in my arsenal for getting attention. Unfortunately, as an independent author, I do not have the deep pockets of the Big City publishing firms. This means you will not see my book cover on the subway or in TV ads.

(Maybe one day!)

But I do have something much more powerful and effective than that, and it's something those publishers would kill to get their hands on:

A WONDERFUL bunch of readers who are committed and loyal!

Honest reviews of my books help get the attention of other readers like yourselves.

If you enjoyed this book, could you help me write even better books in the future? I will be eternally grateful if you could spend just two minutes leaving a review (it can be as short as you like):

Please use the link below to leave a quick review:

http://ssbks.com/LR3

I LOVE to hear from my fans, so *THANK YOU* for sharing your feedback with me!

Much Love,

~Sara

ABOUT THE AUTHOR

Sara Snow was born and raised in Texas, then transplanted to Washington, D.C. after high school. She was inspired to write a paranormal shifter series when she got her new puppy, a fierce yet lovable Yorkshire Terrier named Loki. When not eagerly working on her next book, Sara loves to geek out at Marvel movies, play games with her family and friends, and travel around the world. No matter where she is or what she is doing, she can rarely be found without a book in her hand.

Or Facebook:
    Click Here
    https://ssbks.com/fb
    Join Sara's Exclusive Facebook Group:
    https://ssbks.com/fbgroup

Printed in Great Britain
by Amazon